VERITAS

EX LIBRIS

MACHEN SOCIETY PRESS

# Six Days

L. Chambers Wright

ISBN: 978-1-967310-26-5

Machen Society Press
11876 Stanley Valley Road
Gate City, Virginia 24251
Contact: Publisher@MachenSocietyPress.com
Website: http://MachenSocietyPress.com

Printed in the U.S.A.

# CHAPTER 1

*Well, it isn't much.*

That thought had been playing on repeat since she signed the closing papers. Now, standing in the gravel drive of her new "home," the understatement hit even harder. A faded vinyl-sided bungalow sat squat and tired against a sun-bleached lawn. It looked like it had given up years ago. But it was hers. Because there was no other choice.

The box in her arms shifted, heavy and awkward. She adjusted her grip and trudged up the cracked walkway. It was the kind of heat that made her skin stick to cardboard, made every movement feel like work. She'd had to downsize everything, her home, her car, her life, since Hal died.

She stepped inside and dropped the box just past the threshold. The air inside the house smelled of dust, aged linoleum, and forgotten corners. The living room was mostly empty, save for a few boxes and the scratchy echo of her own breathing. She turned and went back for another load.

The truth was simple: one income couldn't support a mortgage, two car payments, and grief... not in a town like this, where jobs were few and far between, and the good ones were mostly rumors. If Hal hadn't died, if they hadn't been in that wreck, they'd still be making it. Maybe they'd still be laughing at bad TV reruns in their too-big living room with the dog snoring between them. *Poor Amelia.* Their border collie had been in the car with them that night.

But the wreck had changed everything.

She still saw the cops visiting her in the hospital. "We're so sorry..." It haunted her. She saw them every time she closed her eyes that first week. Gradually, she saw them less. Now, just a few times a day.

Six months. That's all it had taken for her life to unravel. After the insurance company paid and the hospital took its cut, she couldn't even think about relocating. She was barely treading water.

Selling Hal's truck had gutted her. He loved that truck. Was proud of it like it was a third member of the family. It had taken them years to be able to afford it, years of cutting corners, skipping vacations, and buying off-brand cereal. Paying off both the car and the truck had felt like finally arriving. Then the accident happened. She thought selling the truck would help more. The house still went on the market before she could bring herself to pack.

She set the next box beside the others and let out a breath. At least she'd managed to sell both the truck and the house at once. That had covered buying this place outright. Smaller. Older. Manageable. Maybe even enough to stay out of the red if she got lucky.

There was some life insurance left. Not much. Barely enough to limp along during her unpaid leave from work. The first three months after the wreck were a blur of painkillers, physical therapy, and sobbing into Hal's shirts. Then came the second leave... to move, to try again.

Of course, "paid leave" didn't exist where she worked. The company handed out platitudes about "family first" and "self-care," but the moment you stepped away from your desk, you didn't get a paycheck. There was always a catch.

The sun hung high above her, mocking with its cheer. Blue sky, birdsong, neighbors' dogs barking down the block, none of it touched her. She wasn't drowning anymore, not exactly. But she wasn't swimming either. She was just... floating. Hollowed out. Going through the motions of being alive.

She still heard him. Still saw him. Hal in the doorway. Hal in the car. His laugh carried in the static of the kitchen radio. She'd been in that car with him. Her body walked away, bruised and bloodied. His didn't.

Sometimes, she still wished she hadn't either.

In the beginning, memories wrapped around her like a blanket, soft, warm, and safe. It felt like love, like he was still close. But over time, that blanket grew heavier, suffocating. The memories stopped comforting and started clinging. And yet, she couldn't stop reaching for them.

Grief had a rhythm; Dr. Tanaka had told her. A strange, unpredictable rhythm. The hallucinations, auditory, sometimes even visual, weren't uncommon. Just the mind trying to make sense of loss.

She carried the last box inside and stacked it by the kitchen entry. These were the personal things, the mementos, the private grief-stained fragments of a life she used to have. The movers had handled the furniture and most of her belongings earlier that morning, but she couldn't let anyone else touch these.

She wasn't healed. Not from the wreck. Not from the loss. Not from the disorientation that came with realizing your entire life vanished in a second. She could barely move a home, even a small one like this. Hiring a moving company had been a necessary expense, even if it left her with another bill she didn't want to face. A bullet bitten.

She stood in the center of the living room and looked around. This was home now. It didn't feel like it.

The house had the bones of an American Craftsman. The pitched roof, the covered porch, the promise of charm, but somewhere along the line, any sense of *craftsmanship* had been choked out by bad renovations and cheap materials. It was all vinyl siding and hollow doors. Even the windows felt like an afterthought.

Her old kitchen had real wood floors, glossy and golden in the light. Here, she had linoleum. Yellowed, cracked, stained with patterns that might've been floral once but now looked like moldy camouflage. The designs had faded into abstract olive smudges and blackish shadows. No amount of scrubbing would revive them.

Every room needed something, paint, wallpaper, flooring... a good exorcism. The windows rattled in their frames. The plumbing wheezed. The wiring hissed if you plugged in too many things at once. The roof had more patches than shingles. She half expected to find duct tape and string holding the place together. Or chewed gum.

She should've gone with the mobile home.

The living room paneling was the worst of it. In some

spots, it had turned nearly black. Streaks ran down the walls like smoke damage. She couldn't tell if it was mildew, dirt, or just years of neglect. She grabbed a cloth, soaked it in cleaner, and wiped a small square near the baseboard.

Underneath, a warm pecan tone emerged, almost glowing. Just one clean spot in a sea of soot. Tempting to paint over the whole thing and call it fixed, but she knew better. Paint would peel right off in months. The wall needed more than cosmetics. The whole house did.

As she straightened, something creaked above her.

Not the usual groan of old wood, but a soft, deliberate sound... like a footstep on the ceiling. She paused, listening. Nothing followed. Just the quiet hum of the fridge kicking on in the kitchen.

Mice, probably. Or the house settling.

Still, a chill crawled up the back of her neck, just under the hairline. She rubbed it away and stepped back from the wall.

The air felt different now. Not colder, exactly, but shifted, like someone had just walked through the room and left a faint wake behind them. She turned slowly, looking over her shoulder.

Empty. Of course. Still, as she moved toward the kitchen to unpack, the clean patch of wall seemed to watch her go.

# CHAPTER 2

Moving into their old house hadn't felt this hard. She leaned her hip against the counter, a half-unpacked box at her feet. Downsizing was supposed to be simpler. Less to manage. Less to maintain. But the truth of it pressed in harder than she expected.

This house was smaller, yes, but no less demanding. If anything, it felt needier. She wondered if a larger fixer-upper would've been the better choice. At least then the mess would've felt proportionate to the space.

She grabbed a dishrag and started scrubbing the already-clean counter again. Dr. Tanaka called the move a "therapeutic reset." A new chapter. But she couldn't stop wondering if it was just another bad decision dressed up in therapy-speak. Every creak in the floor, every crooked cabinet hinge, felt like a small betrayal.

She hadn't thought about how physical a move would be. Not until it was too late. Hal would've known. He would've planned for it. He had always handled the heavy lifting, literally. He was the kind of man who made moving refrigerators look easy. Who never got tired. Who never left things undone.

She shook her head. *No.* That kind of thinking had to stop. Hal was gone. It didn't matter what he had been, because what he was now... was gone.

From below, the scratching noise came again.

She froze, hand on the sink edge. It had started that morning, a dry, persistent scrabble behind the basement door. Maybe mice. Probably mice. It had been off and on, never long, never loud. Just enough to put a pulse of tension in her shoulders.

An exterminator could deal with it. Eventually. Money was the bigger problem. The list of immediate needs was already overwhelming. The list of possible "eventual" necessary repairs stretched into infinity. She conceded to a temporary truce: if the broken pieces pretended to be whole, she would pretend not to notice.

Box after box, she worked robotically, opening, unpacking, flattening, tossing. Cups into cupboards. Towels onto racks. Trinkets into drawers. She kept busy, but her mind wandered. The house wasn't much, but maybe it had potential. That had to count for something.

Somewhere, beneath the exhaustion and the grief, there might still be room for hope. She could hear Hal laugh at that, dry, amused. "It's here somewhere, hon. Keep digging."

The sound came again, this time not from the basement.

"Lisa?"

She froze.

The voice was soft. Almost muffled. Not Hal's. And not the gruff bark of Mel, the white-haired mover who'd spoken for the team earlier. This voice was... smaller. Breathy. Not quite right.

She waited, back rigid, listening. Silence.

No second call. No repeat.

She dried her hands and moved cautiously toward the front of the house. Maybe Mel had returned. Maybe he was trying to say something through the door. But when she reached the window, there was no one there.

The street outside was empty, no rumbling engine, no idling van, no flash of movement. Still, she opened the front door and stepped out onto the porch.

No van.

She glanced to the side yard, then walked around to the back. No movers. Not even a hint of tire tracks left in the driveway gravel. Had they left already? She tried to remember when the sound of the van had stopped. That machine didn't go quietly, she would've noticed. But now, the memory felt... wrong. Distant, like trying to recall a dream.

She went back inside, locking the door behind her.

The living room looked more like a warehouse than a home. Stacks of boxes. Furniture half-positioned. The light through the curtains was too bright, too thin, like the sun was trying too hard.

She hated it. All of it. The move, the loneliness, the sheer, grinding ache of being left behind. Sleep was impossible. Food was mechanical. Her thoughts circled the same drain every day. Home wasn't a place anymore.

No matter how much paint she slapped on the walls, no matter how neatly she stacked the books or arranged the couch, it wouldn't matter. The word "home" required more than furniture. It needed people. It needed him. And Amelia. Laughter. Warmth. And she had none of those left. Just her. Just the echo of what used to be.

And now, the whispers.

That's what scared her most.

It meant she might be slipping again.

Auditory hallucinations, Dr. Tanaka had explained, were common in cases of grief trauma, particularly when paired with disrupted sleep, changes in medication, or prolonged isolation. Lisa had experienced them before, in the raw months after Hal's death. But this one... this was different. This didn't sound like her subconscious playing tricks. It didn't sound like Hal. And it didn't sound like her.

She sat down on a box, pressing her fingers to her temples. Maybe she just needed rest. Maybe she was overtired, overworked, overstressed. There was no reason to jump to conclusions. No reason to panic. Not yet.

She wasn't like Uncle Malcolm.

That name sent a tremor through her. She hadn't thought of him in years, her mother's brother, the one no one talked about. The one who heard voices long before the doctors ever found the tumor. They'd written him off as "eccentric" at first. Then "unstable." Then it was too late. She'd promised herself she would never become like that.

The voice was just a blip. A one-off. It didn't matter. Not unless it came again. Not unless it grew bolder. Not unless...

From behind her, near the basement door, came the soft creak of wood under pressure.

She turned slowly.

No one was there. The door was closed. But somehow, without meaning to, she found herself staring at it. Listening again for that scratching. For a voice. For anything.

The house settled. A pop in the wall. A shifting groan from overhead. Still, the air felt too still. Like something had just left the room. Or was still in it, watching from just behind the edge of her vision. She blinked, then rose, hands steadying on her knees.

"No," she whispered to herself. "Not this time."

She wasn't going back to that madness she experienced right after the funeral. She wasn't going to give in. She had enough battles to fight without inviting new ones in. She walked to the kitchen, grabbed a sponge, and returned to scrubbing down the same counter she'd already cleaned twice.

Outside, the wind picked up... light, uncertain. It rattled the branches of the half-dead oak near the porch. Its shadow moved across the front room wall like fingers, stretching slowly.

She didn't look up. She didn't need to.

# CHAPTER 3

It was her house... but not her own. She moved through the space like a ghost haunting herself. Every step felt rehearsed, like she was mimicking the motions of a life that once existed. Nothing came naturally anymore. Not walking, not blinking, not breathing.

This was supposed to be the same house. Same layout. Same bones. But the moment she opened her eyes that morning, something had shifted. Something fundamental.

She blinked away sleep and rubbed at the crust in her lashes. Her heart beat with an uneasy rhythm as she turned a slow circle in the living room. It wasn't the furniture. It wasn't the light. It was everything else. The angles were wrong. The dimensions were off.

The photos on the walls... she'd never seen them before. Strangers stared back at her from glossy frames. A boy in a faded baseball cap. A woman laughing on a porch swing. The carpet, too, thick and gray blue, she didn't remember ever walking on that.

None of it belonged to her. Somewhere deeper in the house, a voice exploded. "I'll teach you."

The words were spat like venom, low and seething, just before they built into a thunderous bellow: "You'll see when I'm through with you... nobody fucks with Mitchell Owen!"

She froze. The voice reverberated through the walls like they weren't made of wood and plaster but something alive and fragile. She backed away instinctively, but her feet pulled her forward, slow and stiff, as though her body wasn't under her command.

Crying followed... two voices overlapped. A woman. A child. Ragged, terrified sobs. "I'll show you what happens when you cross me." The man ranted, words sharp and fast. It was kind of amazing, if it wasn't so horrific. He didn't even stop to breathe. Obscenities folded into threats and the air grew heavier with each step she took toward the bedroom hallway.

It was darker than it should've been. Shadows clung to the walls like oil. The usual dull amber glow from the bathroom nightlight was gone. The air felt damp, like something was rotting behind the drywall.

She walked down the narrow hall like she was sinking into it. The plaster walls bowed inward as if the house were breathing shallowly around her. The third bedroom door... the farthest one... was shut. A thin, unnatural line of white light traced the entire frame, glowing just enough to etch its shape in the dark.

She had no idea what was happening inside her house. This wasn't grief. This wasn't Hal. He had nothing to do with this. This... was something else.

Claustrophobia set in fast and sharp. The house tightened around her ribs like a vise. The hallway warped inward, pressing on her sides, and the ceiling felt inches from her scalp. The floor seemed to pitch and swell. She couldn't find air. Couldn't think past the constriction in her lungs.

She reached for the doorknob.

Her fingers hovered inches from it... and something hit her in the stomach.

No warning. No impact she could see. But the force knocked the breath out of her. She doubled over in agony. She staggered, hand flailing for the doorframe to steady herself.

She braced, winced, tried to pull herself upright again.

Then another strike... this time to her back, right between the shoulder blades. The pain was white-hot, like bone fracturing under pressure. Her shoulder screamed, and she cried out without sound.

Then... hands.

Two massive, invisible hands gripped her shoulders, one on the injured side. Her breath caught. She was spun like a doll... too fast, too hard... until the hallway whirled and her vision blurred. When she stopped, she was face to face with nothing. No one.

There was no person in the house.

There still wasn't.

But something was there.

A shape... enormous, looming, wrong. It moved like fluid shadow, its edges frayed and pulsing. There was no face, no form, only a presence that filled the space like tar. Malevolent. Radiating cold, deliberate hate.

She whimpered.

The shape tilted forward. Its top half leaned unnaturally close to her face. She couldn't move. Couldn't scream. Her muscles had turned to stone. The hands still held her, though she couldn't see them now... just the weight, the crushing grip.

Her feet left the floor.

She stared down. She watched her toes dangle above the carpet she didn't recognize. She rose higher. Her lungs locked. No oxygen. No sound. Pins and needles exploded across her skin. Her limbs twitched helplessly.

She wanted to scream. Her mouth opened. But breath wouldn't come. The figure held her suspended. Then, without warning... it dropped her.

Her body slammed to the floor with a thud that shook through her bones. And everything went black.

# CHAPTER 4

She opened her eyes to a thin blade of sunlight slicing through the blinds. It painted her cheek with pale gold. The floor beneath her was hard and cold. For a moment, she had no idea how she got there. She was face-down beside her bed.

She groaned, rolled slowly onto her back, and winced. Her arms throbbed with dull pain, stiff and sore like she'd been in a fight.

There were no bruises, no marks, but it felt like there should be. Her cheek ached where it must have struck the floor. She sat up in slow increments. Her joints cracked in protest. Her breath came shallow. The whole night felt more like a struggle than sleep. She might as well not have slept at all.

She rinsed her face in the bathroom. She caught her reflection and flinched. Her skin was pale, stretched thin across her cheekbones. Her eyes were red-rimmed and unfocused, like she hadn't truly rested in weeks. She dressed without thinking, surrounded by a silence so complete it seemed to hum.

She had to check the hallway. It was the only way to prove to herself that it had been a dream. Just a nightmare. Nothing more. A trick of stress and exhaustion.

Still, she turned on every light she passed, as if darkness itself might cling to her heels. The morning sun outside was bright, unapologetic, but the house remained dim. The walls swallowed light. The corners held on to shadow like it was their natural state. She stopped at the threshold of the hallway. It looked... normal.

Boxes exactly where she left them. The same bland, ugly carpet. The same outdated light fixture with its dull, uneven bulbs. Pictures leaned against the walls, waiting to be hung. Her pictures. No voices. No threats. No impossible shadows.

She approached the last door... the one from her dream... with slow, deliberate steps. It was closed.

Had she closed it?

She couldn't remember. But now, just like in the dream, it was the only door in the house that stayed shut. Even before she moved in, she'd decided this room would be for storage. Something about it had repelled her from the start. The air felt wrong inside, cooler, clammy, like the room belonged to another season entirely. Or another place.

She took a breath, turned the knob, and pushed the door open. Sunlight spilled in through the window. Dust drifted in lazy patterns. Boxes sat in awkward piles just where she'd left them. Old paint peeled on the closet door. The smell was the same dry mustiness every spare room carried.

It was just a room.

Still, she waited. She half-expected the shadow to coalesce again. To drip down from the ceiling like tar. But the house remained still.

She turned away.

Her legs carried her out the back door before she realized she was even moving. She stepped onto the porch and sat hard on the top step. Her bones ached. Her heart thudded without rhythm. She wanted to cry, but it felt like a waste of water. What was the point?

She wasn't ready for anything. Not the move. Not the grief. Not the strange new world that pretended to be her life. All she wanted was the old one back. But that wasn't happening.

Maybe more unpacking would help. Make the space feel like hers. Make her feel real again. Maybe it was the air in the house. Stale, heavy. Like it had held its breath since before she moved in. She tried opening the windows, but the air inside never seemed to move. As if the house held onto it, refused to let it go.

She didn't know what the previous owners had burned on those walls. Nicotine? Soot? Were they cooking meth? Or something even worse? Whatever it was, it still clung. Thick. Greasy. Unwilling to leave.

The backyard was flat and open. It joined with four other lots in a wide rectangle of tangled grass and old fences. It was a relief, no high barriers, no chain link cages. Just yards bleeding into one another like a shared secret. Maybe it meant the neighbors were relaxed. Or maybe nobody cared enough to draw lines.

A flash of color caught her eye.

A bright orange ball bounced into view from the side of the house. A little girl chased after it, maybe four years old. She wore a pink tee with a white anime cat and jeans that dragged at the cuffs. She stopped when she spotted Lisa and stared.

She smiled, lifting a hand. "Hi. Who are you?"

The girl smiled back shyly. "Alida."

"I live here now, Alida. I'm Lisa. Where do you live?"

"Here. On Easton Avenue."

Lisa frowned. "Easton? That's down at the intersection, right?" It was at least two blocks away. Too far for a child this small to be wandering alone.

Alida shrugged. "I don't know." She looked off toward nothing in particular, distracted already.

Maybe she'd been told not to give strangers her address. Maybe she just didn't know it. Still... where were her parents?

"Where are your mom and dad?"

"They're busy." The child's tone was simple, final. She turned back to her ball.

She opened her mouth to say something more, but a massive German shepherd padded calmly into view behind the girl. It walked with an air of authority, not wandering, but escorting. The sight of it brought Lisa an odd relief. Not ideal, but better than nothing.

"Hi, doggie," Lisa said gently.

The dog studied her, then looked back at the girl. His gaze flicked again, measuring. Judging. He ultimately decided she wasn't a threat. He walked forward and sniffed her hand.

"What's his name?"

"Remus," Alida called as she bounced her ball.

Remus licked Lisa's knuckles, then turned as the little girl sprinted around the side of the house. He followed close behind, silent and alert.

She watched until they vanished. And then... nothing. No sound. No bark. No footsteps. No door closing.

She rose slowly, brushing the dust from her jeans. She needed to get busy. Time to act like life was normal again. Like rooms didn't change overnight. Like voices didn't crawl out of the walls. Like shadows didn't lift you off your feet and drop you cold.

The house was waiting for her.

# CHAPTER 5

Three days passed without event. No nightmares. No whispers in the dark. No clawing sounds from the basement. Just silence. Silence was a blessing.

The first morning she woke up without dread clinging to her ribs, she felt almost human. Even the mice, it seemed, had moved on to better lodgings. She smirked to herself. *Smart little bastards.* Did they give up territory because a human moved in... or was the place so dilapidated not even vermin wanted it?

She moved like someone recovering from surgery... slow, medicated, and unsure of where one day ended and another began. The medication dulled everything: grief, exhaustion, the edges of memory. It was like wading through a fog that never lifted... only shifted.

The move hadn't helped like Dr. Tanaka said it would. Not really. It hadn't given her closure, hadn't given her peace. It only reminded her, with every squeaking floorboard and crooked window frame, of how much she'd leaned on Hal. How much his absence warped every aspect of her new life.

No matter how many showers she took, or how strong the coffee, the shadow remained. It lived beneath her skin. It coiled behind her eyes. It whispered in the stillness between tasks. The neighborhood offered little distraction.

It was quiet, almost unnaturally so. Aside from the occasional bark of a dog or hum of a lawnmower, the street remained oddly lifeless. The kind of silence that felt deeper than just peace, it felt staged, like the set of a show that never really started.

Alida appeared now and then. Her beautiful white-blond hair caught sunlight like silver thread. She chased her orange ball through the yards and laughed to herself. Lisa caught glimpses of her, a flash of pink, a blur of movement, but she never came too close again. Not since that first conversation. The girl was sweet, bright, and strangely alone.

Still, not all the neighbors were absent.

Sophia Allan, the elderly widow next door, was the kind of woman who lit up a room just by entering it. Her smile was soft but radiant, and she had the curious ability to make Lisa feel like she'd known her for years. Her presence softened the house, gave it a warmth it hadn't yet earned.

On the second day, she'd shown up with a homemade chocolate pie. The kind with the buttery crust that left your fingers greasy, and your stomach satisfied. Sophia helped organize the kitchen and told stories while stacking pots and pans, like she'd done it a hundred times before. Her company eased the tight knot in Lisa's chest, at least while she was around.

But there was something... curious about her, too.

Sophia never asked questions. She offered stories, but none too specific. Her eyes twinkled, but her smile sometimes lingered just a beat too long. She couldn't tell if it was wisdom, or something else.

She wanted to ask about Alida. About where exactly Easton Avenue was, but the questions slipped away each time, like water through her fingers. Maybe it was better that way. Parents could be touchy about strangers asking questions. And if Sophia was a neighborhood hub, gossip might travel faster than she was ready for.

Still, Easton Avenue stuck in her mind like a splinter. She hadn't seen it on any nearby street signs. It wasn't listed on the neighborhood map. Maybe Alida just got confused. Or maybe Easton was one of those tiny streets tucked off a side road, the kind Google never quite pinned down. She made a mental note to ask. Again.

She settled into the gray recliner in the living room with a coffee in hand. The worn, sagging beast of a chair had followed her through three homes. It was the only piece of furniture that felt right. The fabric had faded, the armrests were frayed, but nothing else came close in comfort.

Boxes still towered like miniature monuments to her

past, but she let them wait. They weren't going anywhere. She leaned back with a groan and closed her eyes for a moment, letting the warmth of the coffee seep into her chest.

Her body ached in new and unfamiliar places. She'd underestimated how punishing unpacking could be. Trash bags, boxes, heavy bins, every lift left its mark. But it was worth it, in small ways.

One corner of the living room now looked like someone was living there. A few shelves had actual books. A lamp stood on a real table, not the floor. It wasn't much, but it hinted at stability. She needed those little victories.

Familiarity was the only thing keeping her from unraveling entirely. The home still felt like it wasn't hers, like it was borrowed or staged. But piece by piece, it was changing. She was changing it. Trying to claim it, even if it resisted her efforts.

She thought back to what the realtor, Donald Ferguson, had said when she first toured the place.

"The family's just eager to sell. It's been empty for years. They want it gone. The job market around here's pretty rough. Housing doesn't move much anymore."

She hadn't thought much of it at the time. Houses sit empty all the time in towns like this. Quiet places that clung to the edge of relevance. But now, the comment had a weight she hadn't considered. *Years empty. No tenants.* No upkeep. No neighbors curious enough to step in.

The silence here wasn't just quiet.

It was expectant.

She glanced out the front window and half-expected to see Alida again. But the yard was empty.

The shadows in the hallway seemed to stretch a little longer than before. The air inside the house felt thicker, like the walls were holding something in.

She took another sip of coffee and closed her eyes again, just for a moment. Three quiet days. Maybe it meant she was healing. Or maybe it was just the calm before the next storm.

# CHAPTER 6

It hadn't felt like this when she and Hal bought their first house. Back then, everything had a shimmer to it, even the chores. They'd laughed through late nights painting walls and ordering pizza on the living room floor.

There'd been arguments, of course, real ones, stupid ones, but even those had an edge of warmth. There was something sacred in having someone to argue with.

She pulled the recliner's lever and let the footrest clunk into place. The old chair groaned beneath her, but it held. She exhaled and stared at the ceiling.

All the bad days with Hal had still been better than this... this hollow, quiet version of life. Even paradise would be unbearable without him, not that she'd know. Life since his death had been a long, gray ordeal. She'd lost everything: her sense of self, her stability, her health. Her home. Her desire for... anything, really.

They never had children. It just hadn't worked out before the accident. And now, even the thought of trying with someone else felt offensive. Wrong. Her heart was still married. Still tethered. She hadn't even mourned her Amelia's death. There wasn't room.

There would be no one else. Not for her. Two days. That's all she had before work started again.

The thought sat like a lead weight in her stomach. She wasn't ready. Not for meetings or deadlines or office chatter. She was raw. Tender in ways people couldn't see. Her body still ached from the move, from exhaustion, from grief that never seemed to give her no more than a few feet of space. She just wanted to sleep.

She pushed herself up and turned toward the bedroom. A nap. Just an hour, maybe two. The world could wait.

A light knock broke the silence. She paused.

Not loud, not rushed... just there, sudden and soft.

She turned slowly, her breath catching for no good reason. "Coming," she called, walking toward the door.

She opened it.

No one stood there.

The porch was empty. Mist hung in the air like breath on glass, the remnants of rain making the world look blurred around the edges. Trees shifted gently, leaves slick and dripping.

Lisa sighed. *Great. Pranksters.*

Maybe that's why the house had come so cheap. She hadn't thought to dig too deep into its history. In retrospect, maybe she should have. But she hadn't been able to think clearly in months. Every decision had come through a haze lately.

She closed the door, turned back toward the hallway. *Knock.* Same pressure. Same softness. She froze. Her hand hovered over her chest. She opened the door again.

Alida stood there, alone.

The mist swirled around her bare legs. Today she wore a yellow sundress, and her hair was tied in tight pigtails. She looked like something out of a vintage photograph, delicate, almost too bright for the world around her.

Lisa knelt, eye-level.

"Honey, what are you doing out here? You'll catch the flu."

Alida's face remained calm. "I think my doll fell into the drain. Can you help me?"

"Of course," she said instinctively, standing. She followed the girl to the edge of the driveway, where the metal grate of the storm drain waited in a slick puddle of water.

She knelt and peered into the opening. "Where did you last see...?" She looked up. Alida was gone.

The mist thickened in the air around her, quiet and still. There was no sign of the little girl. No splashing footsteps. No laughter. No Remus.

She stood quickly, scanning the yard. Her heart picked up. There was no way the girl had vanished in five seconds. She couldn't have run off that fast. Not without sound. Not without a trace.

"Alida?" she called. Her voice echoed faintly in the stillness.

Nothing.

Maybe she wasn't supposed to be out. Maybe she ran home when she saw her parents watching. Maybe Remus was around the corner, waiting.

She frowned, her pulse still racing. Her eyes flicked back to the storm drain. She didn't see a doll. Just shadow and water. But the grate looked... older than it should have. Older than the rest of the street. Its metal was dark, almost scorched looking. Too dark for rain.

She stepped back. *Let her parents find the doll.* She turned and walked toward the house. The door creaked as she pulled it open and stepped inside. The house welcomed her with its usual silence.

She didn't know why, but the mist clung to her skin longer than it should have.

# CHAPTER 7

She still had a little while left to enjoy her new home. *Enjoy.* The word didn't sit quite right in her mind. Not yet. But maybe all she needed was rest, real rest, the kind that softened the edges. Maybe she needed to feel that elusive thing people called *sanctuary.*

It was an alien feeling that wore her down the most. Grief was one thing. Constant unfamiliarity was another. Every room, every smell, every texture in this place felt slightly off. Even the food didn't taste right. Her bed, a high-end mattress, barely a year old, felt like it was made of stone.

Grief warped everything. It rewired the senses. Even comfort became foreign. She stepped inside and nudged the front door shut behind her.

From the rear of the house, she heard laughter. Light. Musical. A child's laughter. She moved toward it, through the narrow hallway and into the kitchen. She paused at the back door, listening. The sound trailed off like a fading bell. Gone.

She looked out the windows and scanned the backyard. No flash of yellow sundress. No orange ball. No sign of Remus.

Either she was the target of a remarkably persistent trick, or Alida really was the happiest child in the world.

Outside, the sky was the color of wet concrete. Thick clouds choked out all sunlight, but still, children didn't care. Gray skies meant nothing to them. They carried their own weather, and it was always summer.

Lisa turned and headed toward the laundry room. The light in there was dim and sterile, the walls still bare. She began placing the detergent and fabric softeners on the wire shelf above the washer and dryer.

Then... scratching.

She paused, hand halfway to the bleach bottle. The sound came again, low and quick, from the far-right corner of the room.

She knelt slightly and peered behind the dryer, but nothing moved. The sound wasn't coming from behind it. It was inside the wall.

"Shit."

She leaned forward until her torso rested on the closed lid of the washer. *Rats. Great.* First the scratching in the basement. Then the laundry room. There were probably roaches in the kitchen and termites chewing their way through the joists.

*If Hal had been here...* He would've noticed. Would've known to check for that kind of thing. Would've laughed it off as no big deal and gone to get the traps. She wouldn't have been alone in it. Wouldn't have made the desperate leap for stability that led her to this place.

She closed her eyes. Her forehead rested on her crossed arms. The machine was cold beneath her. Hard. Impersonal. She didn't want to organize anymore.

She didn't want to make this place livable. She wanted to go home. Not this home, the real one. The one with Hal in it. The one with shared laughter and arguments over which takeout to order. The one where grief hadn't stolen the color from the world. But that house was gone. That life was gone.

She stood and walked out without looking back.

*Why me?*

The question looped endlessly. Why did she have to go through this? At her age? So many women at work had been married for twenty years or more, their lives still neatly intact. Why were they spared? Why did she lose her husband in the blink of a moment?

The universe never offered explanations. Only silence. She collapsed onto the bed and pulled the blanket halfway up her chest. She didn't want to think anymore. She didn't want to exist in a world that kept taking.

She closed her eyes. Sleep. That's all she wanted. A sharp thump jolted her back to consciousness.

Her eyes flew open. She lay still, listening. The sound had come from somewhere nearby. Floor or wall, she couldn't tell. Her pulse ticked up a notch.

Maybe the rats had finally chewed their way in.

She lay there, waiting. Listening for squeaks, for the quick scurry of claws across linoleum. Nothing.

As long as they stayed out of her grandmother's china, they could have the kitchen. They could take the whole damn house.

None of it mattered.

She stared at the ceiling, her body still, her mind fraying at the edges. And in the heavy, motionless air, she thought she heard the faintest echo of laughter again, just a breath of it.

Then silence.

# CHAPTER 8

"How are we today, Lisa?" Dr. Kojimura Tanaka leaned forward and gently examined one eye, then the other. His touch was light, clinical. The fluorescent light overhead hummed softly.

"Are you feeling better since the move?" he asked and returned to his stool with his usual practiced calm.

"No, not really, Dr. Tanaka." She tried to keep her voice steady, neutral, but the heaviness leaked through anyway. There was no point pretending. If she was going crazy, she was going crazy. Lying wouldn't change it.

"I still can't break out of it," she said. "It's a different house, but everything feels the same. Like I just moved the grief with me."

She glanced around the office. The Sumi-e paintings on the walls, black ink on pale rice paper, were beautiful in a way that didn't demand attention. Their quiet elegance seemed to suggest balance was possible. Somewhere.

"It's not going to happen overnight, Lisa. Don't pressure yourself." He rolled closer, resting his clipboard on his knee. "Are you still experiencing hallucinations?"

"I'm not sure."

Dr. Tanaka raised an eyebrow, pen paused mid-air. "How so?"

Her mind flitted through recent memories like a shuffled deck, moments pulled out of time, difficult to explain. The knocking with no one there. The girl and her dog, who appeared and vanished at will. The voice in the hall. The dreams that bled into waking.

"I've had several... *incidents*. I've heard knocking, loud, clear, but when I open the door, no one's there. I've heard someone call my name, but it's not a voice I recognize. There's scratching in the walls. Probably rats, I guess."

He nodded slowly, jotted a note, and said, "That last one sounds like a job for an exterminator."

He smiled faintly but didn't dismiss the rest. "The voices are trickier. Could just be stress. Or... you mentioned pranksters, maybe?"

"Sure," Lisa said, though her tone lacked conviction. "Could be. Kids being stupid. I didn't research the neighborhood before I moved. I didn't think to. I wasn't thinking clearly, to be honest. I felt like I was losing it in the old house, and this one's not much better."

"Maybe it's not the house," Dr. Tanaka said gently. "Maybe it's you."

He held up a hand before she could respond. "That's not a judgment, Lisa. It's an opportunity. When something major happens in life, a loss like yours, there's a window. A moment where we're cracked open. That's when we can really look at what's underneath. Who we are. What we need. The circumstances don't need to be perfect for healing to start."

She nodded quietly, unsure whether that was comforting or just another weight to carry.

"How much longer are you off work?" he asked.

"I'm supposed to go back tomorrow."

"I'll write you an extension," he said. "Return next Monday."

Relief flared in her chest, quick, guilty. She needed the time. But she also couldn't afford to take it.

"I appreciate that," she said softly. "I know grieving takes time. I know I'll have bad days and mood swings. I just didn't expect the strange episodes. I don't know what's real anymore. I don't want this to interfere with my job. I can't afford it."

"Grief is a shapeshifter," he said. "For some, it's a weight. For others, a fog. Sometimes it walks right beside you. Sometimes it's hiding in the mirror. The mind protects itself however it can. And sometimes that means disconnection. Distortion."

He made another note in her file. "Have you met any new neighbors?"

"Just one. Sophia Allan. She's a widow, too."

"That could be good for you. Have you spent much time with her?"

"A little. She helped me unpack the kitchen. She's nice."

"Maybe you should visit her. Share a few thoughts. She might need someone to talk to, too."

Lisa hesitated. "Lonely..." she said with a dry laugh. "That makes me sound like a kid. You never really think adults get lonely."

"You'd be surprised," he said without looking up from his notes. "Childhood is a brief chapter. There are more lonely adults in the world than lonely children."

The words sat heavily in the room. A strange silence bloomed after them. She shifted on the exam table, her hands folded in her lap. Outside, the branches of a tree tapped against the window. She looked at the ink paintings again, how the brushstrokes flowed like thought itself, fluid and intentional.

"Do you think I'm crazy?" she asked, her voice barely above a whisper.

He didn't answer immediately. "No," he said finally. "I think you're grieving. But I also think... the line between grief and something deeper can be very thin. So, let's keep talking. And let's keep watching."

She nodded.

As she left the office and stepped into the hallway, she felt the weight shift slightly. Not gone. But acknowledged.

Somewhere behind her, the tree tapped again against the glass. But she hadn't seen any trees outside when she came in.

# CHAPTER 9

Dr. Tanaka had made a good point. Sophia had already been through all of it. The grief, the silence, the long hollow spaces where a husband used to be. She said her husband died twenty years ago.

She had no idea how someone survived that kind of time without the person they loved most, but somehow Sophia had. Maybe it would help to talk to someone who understood. She didn't want to be a burden, but maybe... maybe it wouldn't hurt to lean a little.

Tanaka hadn't seemed particularly worried when she told him about the knocking, the scratching, or the voice calling her name. That should've brought some comfort.

It didn't. Maybe it really was the house settling. Maybe it was rats. Still, her thoughts returned, again, to Uncle Malcolm. By the time the doctors realized what was happening, it was too late. Early-onset dementia had already sunk its claws in. One day, he turned on the gas stove and walked away. He forgot to light the pilot. The fumes nearly killed him.

After that, he never really came back.

He'd always been a little scattered... just a little odd. No one thought it was more than forgetfulness. The doctors said if they'd caught it just a year or two earlier, there might've been hope. His shadow lingered in her thoughts, long and uninvited.

If there were mice in the walls, shouldn't there be signs? Shredded paper, droppings, chewed cords, something? But there was nothing. No trace. No physical proof. Just sound, and silence after. Always that silence. *Maybe they clean up after themselves*, she thought wryly as she left the office.

The drive home stretched like a bad dream. Every green light seemed to wait for her car to approach, only to flash red. She gritted her teeth, hands tight on the wheel, her head buzzed.

The overcast sky hadn't budged. *So much for the sunny*

*afternoon the news promised.* The clouds hung low and bloated, thick as smoke. It had been days since sunlight truly touched anything. Everything was steeped in gray, a world drained of color and time.

As she pulled into her driveway, something caught her eye. A small figure darted around the back of the house. Quick. Barely visible through the mist. Alida?

She parked and grabbed her bag. She missed seeing the girl and Remus. Their play reminded her of something lost and unreachable, laughter, innocence, something that once belonged to her.

She reached for the key. The front door opened before she touched it. Her heart stopped.

She stood frozen, staring at the doorknob. It creaked open an inch further, slow and deliberate. No wind. No movement behind it.

She held her breath and stepped back. "Hello?" she called into the house. Her voice echoed faintly, unanswered.

She turned on her heel and moved quickly back to the car. Her fingers shook as she retrieved her phone and dialed 9-1-1. She turned on the engine and the radio. The sound grounded her while she waited.

Ten minutes later, a patrol car pulled into the driveway. She stepped out under the cover of her umbrella. "Hello, officer."

The man approached with a polite nod. "Good afternoon, ma'am. You called about a break-in?"

"I think so. I just moved in. I went out this morning and when I got back, the front door opened before I could unlock it. I know I shut it tightly before I left."

"Stay here," he said, hand resting on his belt. He walked through the door, disappearing into the house.

Minutes passed.

She nearly called out to him when he finally returned, reappearing in the hallway. "I don't see anything out of place," he said. "Windows and back door are locked. No sign of forced entry. But you should check around... see if anything's missing."

She stepped inside, her stomach tight. They moved

through the rooms together. Her jewelry was untouched. The television sat exactly where it had been. The laptop, her grandmother's china, everything of value remained.

"Are you sure you didn't leave it ajar?" he asked as they returned to the door. "Older doors swell in this kind of damp weather. Makes 'em tricky."

She nodded, but her jaw clenched. "Maybe."

He smiled politely. "Doesn't hurt to be cautious. You did the right thing, calling us. Always report it. Just in case."

"Thank you, officer. I'm sorry if I wasted your time."

He shook his head. "Not at all. That's what we're here for."

She watched as he pulled out of the driveway and disappeared down the street. The house seemed to grow darker the moment he left.

She reached for the front door. It opened smoothly. No sticking. No warping. She closed it. Opened it again. Easy. She remembered locking it that morning. Pulling it shut. She was certain.... Or was she thinking of the day before?

A cold thought pricked the back of her mind: *Uncle Malcolm used to leave doors open, too.* She tried to push it away. It didn't help. The idea lingered like fog. She didn't want to wonder if it was her mind slipping...or something else entirely.

She already had enough to worry about.

# CHAPTER 10

She needed to visit Sophia. The white-haired woman next door seemed like the type who carried quiet wisdom, someone who'd lived through the kind of loss Lisa was still choking on. Sophia had survived it for decades. Maybe just being around someone like her would help shift her out of the fog she hadn't been able to shake.

Nobody at work had called. Not even once. She wasn't surprised. They hadn't said much after Hal died, either. A few of his coworkers came to the funeral. A couple of cards. One flower arrangement.

Her coworkers hadn't done anything at all. It was easy to have friends when you didn't need them. Sadly, friends were never like those on tv or in movies.

She grabbed her keys and locked up. She checked each door on reflex. Then she stepped outside into the cool, clean air. The rain had finally scrubbed away the thick humidity. Clouds still clung to the sky, but the light felt easier, like the storm had cleared something beyond the weather.

Sophia's bungalow looked nearly identical to hers in structure, but not in spirit. Its white siding gleamed, even under the gray sky, and the garden along the walkway was neatly kept. Lived-in. Loved.

She walked up to the porch and knocked. A warm voice floated from somewhere near the kitchen: "Who is it?"

"It's Lisa," she called.

The door opened quickly, and Sophia beamed. "My word, this is unexpected. How wonderful of you to stop by."

Inside, the house was exactly what she'd expected, cozy, filled with scent and sound. They moved into the living room, still chatting about nothing in particular. Lisa sank into an overstuffed sofa that reminded her of her grandmother's. It welcomed her like a hug.

Sophia moved easily between the kitchen and living room, returning with iced tea and slices of lemon cake. Her steps were slow, but never hesitant.

Framed photographs lined every wall, sepia portraits from the early 1900s, washed-out color snapshots from the '70s, Polaroids, digital prints. The house wasn't run by a television. It didn't even need one. Conversation was the entertainment.

After a lull in the chat, Lisa decided to ask. "How long did it take you to grieve for your husband, Sophia?"

Sophia's hands paused on her teacup. Her clear blue eyes lost a bit of their light. "My dear," she said softly, "I still grieve for him." Lisa sat up straighter.

"That's something many new widows don't understand," Sophia continued. "The grief never really leaves. Not completely. There's always that longing tucked away somewhere. Even remarrying won't erase it... and it shouldn't. When you've loved someone that deeply for that long, it becomes part of you. The better the marriage, the harder the grieving."

She looked at Lisa, her gaze steady. "Are you having a hard time?"

"I'm afraid so." The words felt small. Inadequate.

She didn't want to pour everything out. Sophia didn't need to hear the dark parts, the monster in the hallway, the dreams, the voices. Still, she couldn't say nothing. The look Sophia gave her made that impossible.

"How so?" the older woman asked gently, sipping her tea, never breaking eye contact.

Lisa swallowed. "I've just had so many emotional shifts. I can't get out from under the shock... or the pain. Most days, I feel numb. But there's this deep ache underneath. It's like I'm hurting and not feeling it all at once." There. Neatly packaged. Truthful enough without spilling too much.

Sophia nodded slowly. "You think that isn't normal?"

Lisa bit the inside of her cheek and nodded again. She hated how quickly emotion rose when someone actually listened.

Sophia set her glass down with a soft clink. "You know,

all this talk of psychological profiles and timelines for grief... it's nonsense. The professionals mean well, but most of the widows I've known over the years would've been institutionalized if they told the truth about their process."

Lisa blinked.

"I knew a woman," Sophia went on, leaning back in her navy rocker, the one with delicate lace doilies on the arms, "who kept her husband's ashes on the mantel. Every day, she talked to him like he was still there. For decades. And you know what?"

"What?"

"She lived a full, happy life. Worked, volunteered, raised grandchildren. No one ever knew about her habit. It was just what helped her. That was her way."

Lisa listened, transfixed.

"Most of us move through grief in our own way, at our own pace," Sophia said. "We aren't case studies. We're people. You may process this like someone else, or not at all like anyone. That's all fine. Your mind and body will sort it out when they're ready. Don't force yourself. Life returns, bit by bit. When it's time."

Lisa looked down at her tea, unsure of what to say. But something inside her felt just a little less heavy.

# CHAPTER 11

Sophia made more sense in five minutes than Dr. Tanaka had in months. She smiled faintly; warmth rose in her chest. "Thank you, Sophia. That really helps."

Sophia nodded. "Doctors mean well, but most are terribly naïve. Experience is the greatest teacher. Unfortunately, those who are in the middle of learning it firsthand are often labeled as broken. Or worse."

Their conversation drifted after that, soft and unhurried. The room was a gentle cocoon of quiet talk, the occasional clink of porcelain, and the faint hum of birdsong outside the open window. She found herself relaxing, truly relaxing, for the first time in weeks.

Then she saw it.

Through Sophia's frilly sheers, a flash of orange, Alida's ball. The little girl chased it across the opposite side of the yard, Remus close behind her. She smiled without thinking.

"Sophia, have you ever heard of a child named Alida?"

The shift was instant.

Sophia's eyes became cold. Not guarded, cold. The softness in her face vanished.

"We don't discuss her or her family," she said flatly. "You shouldn't either." The room chilled. The comfort dissolved, like someone had thrown open a door to a snowstorm.

She froze. "Oh. I'm sorry. I didn't mean to—"

"No, no," Sophia said quickly, but her voice was tight. She set her cup down carefully, both hands on the handle. "I know you're new here, Lisa. But please. Believe me when I tell you, you don't want to know about that family. Their story is deeply unhappy. And it will only bring you unhappiness in turn. Focus on yourself. On healing. Get plenty of rest. And do not speak of her again."

She nodded, her heart suddenly pounding. *Too late,* she

thought. She'd already spoken to the girl. Had conversations. Shared moments. But she said nothing.

She changed the subject, and Sophia responded civilly, but something had changed. Her posture never quite relaxed. Her tone stayed measured. The grandmotherly warmth that had wrapped around the room like a blanket was gone. The room felt... alert now. Like it was listening.

She forced herself to finish her tea. They made casual conversation again, but Sophia's smile never quite reached her eyes.

When she left, Sophia wrapped a piece of lemon cake in wax paper for her. "For later," she said, handing it off with a careful nod.

Lisa stepped outside and glanced toward her own house. She hoped no one was watching. A sudden, irrational fear flickered, what if the neighbors were watching? What if the wrong question had already branded her? Ostracized for acknowledging a child.

She hadn't even been accepted by this community, but already she could feel herself drifting toward exile.

*Ridiculous.* She was an adult. They couldn't make her ignore a child. She wouldn't. Maybe no one liked Alida's family. Maybe something awful had happened, long ago. But that wasn't the girl's fault. You don't get to choose your parents. She was just a child, and she didn't deserve to be treated like a pariah.

She resolved, then and there, to look into it. Just a little. A name, a date, anything that could help ease the itch in her mind.

When she returned home, she found the kitchen door ajar. Her stomach dropped. She knew she'd locked it. Just like she'd locked the front door the other day, before she found it wide open. She stood frozen for a beat on the back steps. Her hand trembled slightly on the knob.

She didn't call the police this time.

She stepped inside alone.

The house was quiet. Still. But something in the air felt off, like it had been disturbed. Touched. She moved slowly from room to room. Nothing was missing. Nothing appeared moved.

*Maybe it's nothing*, she thought. But it didn't feel like nothing.

Maybe it was pranksters. But if it wasn't, she needed to be prepared. She couldn't afford to be caught off guard. Lisa headed straight for the storage room and dug through a box until she found the disposable 35mm camera she and Hal had bought the day before the wreck. She would use her phone, but her photos never turned out good.

She started with the china, carefully noting the embossed gold trim and tiny manufacturer marks beneath each piece. Then her jewelry, her stereo, her laptop. Her grandmother's locket. One item after another, cataloged and captured. She photographed every room, corners, windows, shelves. Evidence. Just in case.

When she finished, she locked up again. Every door. Every window. Then she drove to Photos in a Flash, the little one-hour developer near the edge of town. The place hadn't changed in years. It smelled like chemicals and damp cardboard. Film canisters lined the wall behind the register. New cameras, most of them digital, sat untouched in dusty display cases. She handed over the camera. The teenager at the counter promised the prints by tomorrow.

As she walked back out into the gray afternoon, Lisa wondered, faintly, what she'd see in those photos when they came back.

And whether everything in them would still be there.

# CHAPTER 12

The front door was cracked open... again.

She froze on the porch. Her keys dangled in her hand. She gently pushed the door inward and peeked inside. Nothing was disturbed. No overturned furniture. No sign of entry. Still, her skin prickled with unease.

She stepped in and shut the door. She locked it behind her, though it no longer felt like it mattered.

She crossed to her recliner and reached for the lever, then stopped. There was a faint glow in the hallway, a golden light. Not from the overhead fixture. Not from the window. It shimmered along the crack beneath the spare bedroom door, the bad room.

Her breath caught. Maybe the clouds had finally broken, and the last light of dusk was pouring in. That had to be it. Still, she moved cautiously down the hallway, her bare feet silent on the cool floor.

As she neared the door, she realized the light wasn't natural. It didn't shine like sunlight. It glowed, warm, bronze, and unnatural, like the dying embers of something not quite fire. She stopped. Waited. Nothing moved inside.

She scanned the hallway for something, anything, to use as a weapon. She spotted Hal's old baseball bat leaning against the wall, right where she'd forgotten to put it away. Her hand closed around the grip, tight and trembling.

"Hello?" she called softly.

No answer.

She nudged the door open with the end of the bat. It creaked wide, inch by inch. She stepped inside, bracing for something, someone, behind it. But there was no one.

The room was empty. Dim. Still. And the light was gone.

She let out a breath, confused. Had she imagined it? The glow? The warmth? She dropped the bat to the floor, her arms aching from tension. Her back muscles screamed as the adrenaline faded.

The room was cold again. Not cool, cold. It radiated unease. She hadn't spent much time here. The only window looked into Sophia's backyard, and she'd avoided that view from the start. Something about seeing those rows of matching fences made her feel watched.

She shivered.

The air smelled wrong, not foul, not rotted, but... off. Like there should be a scent. The ghost of a bad smell. A phantom odor that didn't exist.

She turned to leave. Something stopped her. She couldn't move.

Her body froze. Her breath halted in her throat. It felt like someone stood behind her, close enough to feel heat that wasn't there. Her heart pounded wildly against her ribs. Her mind screamed the same word over and over: *Run.*

A figure stood at the window. A woman. Motionless. Back turned. Lisa's blood iced.

She had waist-length blonde hair, soft and gleaming. It looked like Alida's. Her jeans were faded. Her T-shirt was once black, now brown with age. The figure whispered something, a breath of words barely audible.

Her voice cracked. "Hello?"

The woman didn't turn. She stared through the glass. She stepped closer.

*"He shouldn't have done it. He shouldn't have done it,"* the figure whispered, again and again. Her voice grew faster, fainter, a chant unraveling into static.

"What did he do?" She whispered. She was only a step behind her now.

Suddenly, the figure spun. "What you did!" she screamed. The room exploded.

She felt the woman's hands slam into her shoulders. Her feet lifted from the ground. She flew backward across the room. She hit the wall so hard the drywall cracked, and the door frame splintered. She collapsed to the floor, pain blooming across her entire body.

She couldn't breathe. Couldn't move.

The woman's scream wasn't human. Not anymore. It echoed with something ancient and broken, like rage turned inside out.

Lisa's eyes clenched shut. She waited for the next strike. But nothing came.

Silence.

When she opened her eyes, the room was empty. The figure was gone.

She stared at the wall, expecting to see the damage, the cracks, the broken door. But everything was intact. Smooth. Untouched.

She whimpered. Crawled to the wall. Ran her fingers over the paint. No dents. No breaks. As if none of it had happened.

She staggered upright, barely able to stand. Pain throbbed through her spine, into her ribs. She limped into the living room and reached for the cordless phone. It slipped from the cradle and crashed to the floor. She picked it up with numb fingers and called Dr. Tanaka's office.

The receptionist tried to put her on hold. She refused. Finally, his voice came through.

"Lisa?" He sounded concerned, and annoyed.

"Dr. Tanaka. I have a very serious problem," she said flatly. Her voice broke. There was no energy left for panic. Only this hollow certainty that something had shifted again. And this time, something knew she knew.

"What happened?" His tone changed instantly.

"I've been meaning to call. But today..." Her breath caught. "I think I was attacked."

"Do you need an ambulance?"

"I... I hope not." Her voice broke on the edge of a sob.

She told him everything, the open doors, the figure, the scream, the fall. The damage that vanished. She recited the details like a police report, as if giving it structure would make it more believable.

When she finished, there was a pause.

"Give me your address," he said at last. "I'm coming by.

It's on my way home. Lie still. Don't do anything else."

She gave it to him, then dropped the phone. It clattered to the floor and lay there, buzzing gently on the carpet. She couldn't bring herself to pick it up.

Outside, she heard Alida's voice rise in a singsong melody.

> The monster's in the closet...
> The monster's in the closet...
> The monster's in the closet...
> Now he's under the bed...

The tune skipped and echoed in Lisa's mind, warped and off-key. She looked toward the window and saw the tip of Alida's head bouncing by. But she couldn't move. Couldn't call out.

She wanted to ask Alida what she meant. What she knew. But her eyes were already drifting closed. It was going to be a long hour.

# CHAPTER 13

She slowly opened her eyes to the low, distant sound of a soft roar. Not mechanical, natural, maybe, like wind in a tunnel. Something moved in the periphery. A shadow shifted across the room. Apprehension bloomed deep in her chest.

*Not again.*

The memory slammed back into her, the shadow from the nightmare, the dream that never really felt like a dream. Her limbs tensed. Her breath caught.

But as her vision cleared, the fluorescent haze sharpened around her. White walls. Machines. The antiseptic smell of plastic and alcohol. She was in a hospital.

Maybe it had all been a dream. Maybe she was back where it all started, after the crash, when Hal had been alive in another room, waiting. She could almost feel that hope again, clawing up from the past.

She tried to sit up. Her back screamed in protest. She dropped back onto the pillow with a sharp breath.

"Lisa?" A voice came through the soft chaos of hospital sounds.

"Yes?" she whispered.

"Do you know where you are?" It was a man's voice. Familiar, but distant.

"In... a hospital?"

"That's right." The voice moved closer. "Do you know why you're here?"

"A car wreck?"

The shadow resolved into a face. Dr. Tanaka stood beside her bed, peering into her eyes with the same practiced calm he always wore. For a moment, she thought it really was back then, that Hal was in the next room, waiting to hold her hand again.

But the moment passed. It wasn't then. And Hal was

still gone.

"Something happened at the house," she said flatly.

"Yes," he replied.

"I hurt my back..."

"You did." He nodded. "Now... can you tell me where the house is?"

"125 Wagner Avenue," she said softly.

"Good. And what do you remember?"

She stared at the ceiling. "I don't want to remember."

"I didn't ask what you wanted to remember, Lisa." His tone didn't budge. "Tell me what you do."

"A woman was in my house. In the back bedroom. I thought she needed help... I approached her, and she turned. She pushed me." Her voice slowed, like she had to step carefully over each word.

"But she wasn't human. Her eyes were black. Bleeding. Her neck was torn open. There was a line around her throat... dark, bruised. She threw me so hard I hit the wall. I saw the drywall crack. The doorframe broke. But when I looked again, it was all gone. Like it never happened."

Dr. Tanaka nodded. "Very good. I have to tell you what I saw."

She braced herself.

"I got to your house and found the front door wide open. You were unconscious on the couch. I couldn't wake you. I called for an ambulance. Lisa, there was no sign anyone else had been there."

She said nothing.

"But your back..." He hesitated, then leaned forward. "Your injuries are extensive. Multiple vertebrae almost fractured. Your left scapula is cracked. You have significant bruising across your back and shoulder. The kind of impact you experienced... it's not the kind someone can cause themselves. And yet..."

"And yet," she said for him.

"There was no damage to the wall. No cracks. No splinters. Nothing."

She let the words sink in. "So now they think I did it to

myself."

He didn't answer directly. "Officers questioned the possibility. They remembered you had called in a false alarm before. But I told them there's no way, no way, you could've done this alone. And not left a trace."

She turned her face toward the white ceiling. It seemed to glow with a sterile purity. Like it didn't belong to any real world.

"I don't care what they think," she whispered. "I know what happened. And you wouldn't be talking like this if you didn't believe some of it."

"I don't know what's happening to you," he said quietly. "But something is. Your injuries are real. Your confusion is real. And your fear."

"I just want it to stop." She cut him off. Her voice wasn't angry. Just exhausted. "I'm not even sad anymore. I'm just... done."

He sat silently for a moment.

"You may need physical therapy," he said at last. "We'll know more in a few days. But I'm extremely concerned about what's been happening since you moved."

She turned toward him. "Did anyone check the doors?"

"The responding officers said moisture might be causing them to swell."

"They weren't swollen," she said flatly. "They opened and closed like new. I remember."

"I checked before I left." He hesitated again.

She saw it, something he wasn't saying. He was going to have her committed. Just like Uncle Malcolm.

Her father's uncle, technically, but he'd always just been "Uncle." The man who'd wandered out in the cold. Who stared at corners and shouted at empty chairs. The one they sent to the "Camp for Woodsy Thinkers," as her family called it. Their polite way of saying "locked away."

Maybe she was next. Maybe she already was.

"Lisa, maybe you should move," Dr. Tanaka said quietly.

She laughed once, too sharply. "Again? You want me to move again?"

"I don't think it's safe."

"I have no choice. I have no money. I shouldn't even be missing work this week. That house was empty for years. It'll take just as long to sell it. And I can't afford another move."

"I can't let you go back."

"Why?" she asked, not out of challenge, but weariness.

"Because I care about you, Lisa." His voice softened. "I've treated you for ten years. I've watched you climb out of dark places before. But this... this house, it isn't helping you. It isn't... neutral."

Her voice was barely a murmur. "What's wrong with it?"

"I can't explain it in scientific terms. I know how that sounds. But the air inside isn't right. The temperature fluctuates strangely. There are cold pockets that don't align with anything physical. The doors don't stay shut, and there's no mechanical cause. And worse...."

"Worse?" she echoed.

"There's a sense of negativity in the home. A... pressure. A presence."

Lisa blinked. "You think my house is haunted?"

"You can laugh. That's fine." He didn't flinch. "I just want you to know what I felt. Not as your doctor. As your friend."

"I appreciate that," she said slowly. "But there's nothing I can do. I don't have anywhere else to go."

He sat back. The silence between them said everything else.

# CHAPTER 14

The conversation dwindled, and Dr. Tanaka eventually left to check on his other patients. She stared at the ceiling long after the door clicked shut behind him.

*Haunted.*

He'd never alluded to anything remotely supernatural before. Not once. Not in ten years of examinations and checkups and medication adjustments. And now here he was, talking about cold spots and negative air like he was reading lines off a ghost-hunting show.

Wasn't that the kind of thing movie producers threw in to sell tickets? Haunted castles. Creepy basements. Screaming women in nightgowns. Her house was hardly the stuff of horror legend. A tired old bungalow with faded vinyl siding and linoleum that peeled in corners. It barely had working plumbing.

So, where the hell was her leading man? The rugged hero who fights off demons with a flashlight and some charm. The one who runs toward the danger and saves the day just before the credits roll?

Nowhere. Just her. Her, a broken recliner, and an invisible force that may or may not exist.

She sighed and shifted slightly. Pain stitched through her spine. Her thoughts spiraled. What other nonsense was coming? Would someone accuse her of being a witch next? Say she hexed Hal?

The idea was ridiculous. And yet, not more ridiculous than the fact that she could describe the face of the woman who wasn't there. That she could still hear the scream. That her body bore bruises from something nobody saw.

If ludicrous was the currency of the day, she had a few claims of her own. Hell, she had a ledger. She closed her eyes.

The numbness returned like a warm, wet blanket. It wasn't comfort. But it was better than pain. Better than memory.

Sometimes, there were benefits to feeling nothing. And she wasn't in a hurry to let them go.

# CHAPTER 15

It was no use. She wasn't listening, no more than anyone else would. So many Western minds recoiled at anything spiritual. It was always the same: if it couldn't be weighed, measured, or bottled, it didn't exist. But spirituality wasn't mystical or magical. It wasn't some vast conspiracy to control the simple-minded.

It was just... part of life. Humans were spiritual beings by nature, for a reason. Primitive people hadn't paused their desperate, exhausting lives to worship the old gods out of boredom. They did it because they needed to. Because even they knew humans were inherently spiritual.

Once upon a time, sound waves were fantasy. Germs were science fiction until the late 1800s. Electricity? Magic. Indoor lighting? Witchcraft. The spiritual realm was no different, just another frontier, not yet mapped.

Something was wrong with Lisa's house. And he knew it. He blamed himself for her being there. Lisa and Hal had been two of his best patients, bright, grounded, respectful. Devoted to one another. Even privately, each spoke as highly of the other as they did together. That kind of marriage was rare.

Grief had destroyed all of that. Lisa had struggled, yes, but she was progressing, even if slowly. And then she moved into that house. From that point on, it was a steady slide downward.

There were things he hadn't told her. Couldn't. He'd nearly been knocked backward when he entered the house, especially that back bedroom. The air there didn't feel wrong, it was hostile. Suffocating. It did not want occupants.

He'd requested radon and carbon monoxide tests. Both came back negative. There was no physical explanation for what he experienced, or what happened to Lisa. No damage to the walls. No shattered wood, no cracked plaster. Her injuries should have left clear evidence. A person doesn't bruise like that, doesn't crack bone, from thin air.

The police couldn't explain it. The EMTs were baffled. But they didn't press it. Maybe because Lisa was a widow. Maybe because no one wanted to deal with anything they couldn't easily close a report on.

The house itself wasn't even in livable condition. The realtor had taken advantage of Lisa's grief, sold her a pile of health hazards with a coat of paint. Water stains had been lazily covered. New ones were already forming. The flooring was unstable. Mold was growing under the sinks, and probably in the walls. Nothing about it met code.

And still, even with all that, those flimsy walls should have splintered under the kind of force it took to cause Lisa's injuries.

He knew construction. He'd spent summers helping his father's crew during medical school. You don't throw someone across a room in a structure like that and leave no evidence behind. And now, he had to reckon with the reality that Lisa wouldn't leave.

Not unless she believed. And she wasn't ready to.

He'd mentioned the girl, once. Just once. That strange little girl Lisa had seen, Alida. But there were no children in the neighborhood by that name. None of the officers had seen a child playing outside the day they responded.

Still, when he mentioned the name to Sergeant Cooper, something in the man's face changed. Drained of color. A hard swallow, averted eyes. The others stayed quiet, but Cooper's reaction stood out. He was rattled. Spooked.

He didn't press it. Not yet. But it stuck with him.

Now, sitting in his office, he typed Lisa's address into the hospital's internal system. Just a hunch. Just to see. There was a note that the road name had been changed recently. He retried with the old name.

Two names appeared almost immediately.

Owen, Morgan
Owen, Alida

He stared at the screen. Morgan's last visit was on September 14, 2012. She was 25 years old. Multiple bruises. A suspected broken arm. She'd been x-rayed and examined. Social Services had been called.

Alida had been there, too. Her visit was recorded that same day. Morgan had been questioned, suspected of abuse, but her injuries were inconsistent with that. They couldn't have been self-inflicted. That seemed to be enough to stall any further action.

And then they were gone.

Their address was listed as 147 Easton Avenue. Just a few streets from where Lisa lived now. Their number was local. Routine visits after Alida's birth, nothing unusual. But the entries ended there. They'd simply vanished.

There was nothing else in the system. No follow-up. No transfer. No official note of moving out of state. Just silence.

He sat back in his chair. He had the feeling he was missing something. Something obvious. Maybe the answers weren't in medical files. Maybe it was time to look elsewhere. Deeds. Police records. Local history.

Whatever had happened there hadn't started with Lisa.

But it might very well end her.

# CHAPTER 16

She lazily opened one eye, then the other. Her head no longer floated near the ceiling like it had earlier, now it was just hovering above the bed. The haze was thinning. The drugs must be wearing off.

Outside the window, the world had dimmed to dusk. Gray-blue shadows crept across the floor. The sterile scent of antiseptic coated the air, clung to her skin, soaked into her gown.

She listened.

Somewhere beyond her room, the faint rhythm of hospital life hummed on: the beep of telephones, murmured conversations from the nurses' station, the distant clap of determined footfalls on linoleum. Reassuring. Routine.

But beneath it all... something else.

Another sound. Softer than the others. Familiar. A child's laughter.

Alida?

Her heart skipped. The laugh echoed faintly down the hallway, bright and girlish and far too familiar. Her body tensed on instinct, but the sharp pain that followed stole her breath. She couldn't move. Not really. Even a twitch sent pain radiating from her spine through her shoulders and down her side.

Then came the sound of a ball bouncing past her door. Just once. She tried to lift her head.

Something lower than the laughter stirred next, barely audible. A sound that didn't belong. A low, distant roar. It might have been the wind, maybe. But the trees beyond the plate-glass window outside her room were still. Motionless.

The footsteps that followed weren't the brisk clicks of nurses or the quiet pads of doctors. They were heavy. Measured. Plodding. Like boots.

She hit the call button. She struggled to breathe through the pain.

Moments later, a cheerful nurse entered the room, pushing a paper cup of medicine on a tray. Her smile was warm. Normal. Comforting.

She watched her carefully.

"Is anyone else in the hall?" she asked. "I thought I heard a kid."

The nurse shook her head. "No, there sure isn't. Visiting hours ended a while ago."

"Thank you."

The nurse turned to leave. She pulled the curtain back to give Lisa a view of the hallway before stepping out. And there she was.

The woman from the house. The one from the bedroom. The scream. The blood-black eyes. She stood directly in the nurse's path.

Lisa's mouth opened to shout, but nothing came out. Her lips barely moved. The nurse froze mid-step, her eyes locked on the grotesque figure in front of her.

The woman's hair, long and golden, once beautiful, suddenly whipped forward, wrapping around the nurse's neck like a noose. Her body lifted into the air, dragged upward as if by some invisible hook.

The woman sobbed, high and keening. Her arms trembled with rage. The nurse kicked, gasped. Her shoes scraped the floor before her body lifted too high to touch it. Her face went purple. Lisa choked on a scream.

"Nurse—!"

And then, everything was gone.

The hallway was empty. The nurse stood at her bedside, calm as ever.

"Yes?" she asked gently. "Is something wrong?"

She blinked. Her heart thudded so hard, she saw the fabric of her gown pulse with each beat.

She forced a smile. "Nothing. I... I thought someone called for me. Bad dream."

The nurse tilted her head slightly. "No, honey. All's

quiet. You're okay." She patted Lisa's hand and slipped out of the room.

She stared at the now-empty doorway. Her father's voice echoed somewhere in the back of her mind, singing that absurd song he made up when she was little:

> Oh, I salute thee, Woodsy Thinkers,
> remember me when you wash your hands.
> The voices you hear, do not appear,
> because they're from the aliens...

He always said it with a grin. Always followed it with, *"Every person in this world is just one misfiring synapse from woodsy thinking, Lisa. Every single one of us."*

She smiled to herself. Not because it was funny. But because it might just be true.

# CHAPTER 17

She wouldn't accept fear, not yet anyway. Even though she felt like she had already fallen from the edge of something deep, and the ground hadn't quite caught her. The sensation lingered like vertigo, a dizziness that made everything feel distant, blurry, suspended. But she wasn't going to let it take her. Not yet.

She needed to focus. She couldn't afford to lose herself to whatever was happening. She tried to push the rising panic away, clinging to the thought that maybe, just maybe, Tanaka was right.

Maybe there was something wrong with the house itself. That would explain the strange occurrences, the unexplained bruising, the weird cold spots in the walls, the constant nagging feeling that something wasn't right. Tanaka didn't seem to think there was anything wrong with her mind, he didn't think she was crazy.

That thought gave her a sliver of relief, like someone had just thrown her a rope. She held on tightly, as if it might pull her back from the edge. But then again, what if he was wrong?

What if she was losing it? What if everything was inside her head? The thought was suffocating, a slow tightening of her chest. She didn't want to be insane. She couldn't be. That was worse than anything, the idea that it was all in her head, that she was imagining the nightmares, the bruises, the suffocating presence in her own home.

But what about the house? What about the noises, the strange air that filled the rooms? The coldness of the back bedroom, the eerie laughter she'd heard, Alida's laughter, and the way things felt wrong in ways she couldn't explain?

She couldn't dismiss it all as nothing. Her mind may

have been playing tricks, but that didn't explain the bruises on her body, the shattered pieces of her back.

The doctors said it wasn't self-inflicted, and she didn't believe that she could do this to herself, even if her mind was cracked. But what if it was the house? What if something in it was pulling at her sanity, manipulating her thoughts and memories?

Neither option seemed possible. Neither felt like a reality she could live with. A haunted house? It sounded absurd. She could almost laugh at the thought if it didn't make her feel nauseous. And yet, deep down, she couldn't shake the gnawing sensation that something wasn't right. Her house was suffocating her, and she didn't know how to escape it.

The drugs still clouded her thoughts, but she had enough clarity to know that if she didn't do something, she wouldn't make it out in one piece. Next time, whatever it was, it wouldn't stop with bruises. Next time, it could break her. Next time, it might snap her neck, or worse, leave her twisted, trapped in her own mind forever. She couldn't let that happen.

She couldn't afford to be passive anymore. She had to face whatever was there, whether it was inside her head or in the house. She had to find out. She had to find a way to break free. Before it was too late.

# CHAPTER 18

She almost convinced herself it had all been a horrible hallucination. Three uneventful nights in the hospital had a way of softening the edges. No apparitions, no spectral voices, no disembodied laughter. Just IV fluids, fluorescent lighting, and the cold, impersonal comfort of antiseptic air.

She packed her few belongings with slow, careful movements, gritting her teeth each time her back tensed. It was the third day. Tanaka had cleared her for discharge. Medically stable.

But "stable" didn't mean anything close to ready. She could barely lift her purse. She couldn't stand long enough to cook. Showering had been an exercise in endurance. And when she thought of climbing the stairs to her front porch or maneuvering into bed without crying out in pain, her optimism shriveled.

The insurance money was nearly gone. Her leave from work had already stretched beyond what she could afford. Another week, possibly more, before she'd be able to return.

And yet... no shadows. No nightmares. No flickers of Alida outside her window. Nothing. It had almost been a vacation. Almost. Now came the hard part, getting to the taxi.

She stepped into the hall, hunched and aching. Her steps were uneven and slow, her shoes whispering against the tile floor. She held her purse against her chest like it might shatter if it swung too hard.

A man turned a corner too quickly and bumped into her. Pain stabbed through her back like lightning. She gasped and stumbled, gripping the wall to keep from falling.

"Oh God, Lisa, I'm so sorry!"

The voice was familiar. She blinked up through the haze of agony. Dr. Tanaka? But not like she'd ever seen him before.

He wasn't wearing his white coat. No stethoscope. No clipboard. Just a crisp white polo shirt and khaki pants. For a moment, she didn't recognize him. He looked smaller somehow. Less clinical. More human.

"Dr. Tanaka?" she said, breathless.

"It's me," he said, smiling. "Just call me Koy. I figured I'd help you get home. I heard you were being discharged. Your car's still at the house, right?"

"That's really kind of you," she said, trying to return the smile. "But I called a cab."

"You shouldn't be walking." He glanced down the hallway, then back at her. "Hang on." He turned and disappeared for a moment, then returned pushing a wheelchair.

"Oh, come on, that's not necessary. I'm sure I can walk...."

"And if someone else bumps into you like I just did?" he gently cut her off. "You have multiple injuries that could worsen. You need to let yourself heal. A nurse should've brought a chair already."

She opened her mouth to argue but closed it. She didn't have the energy. Agreeing meant getting home faster. He helped her into the chair with quiet care, then guided her down the corridor toward the elevators.

"You have groceries at the house?" he asked.

"A few. I figured I'd go out later and... well, you know what happened." She stopped mid-sentence.

Faint. Barely audible. Laughter. High-pitched. Playful. Familiar. Alida. The sound floated up the elevator shaft like a whisper carried on the wind. Her chest tightened.

He looked at her, sharp-eyed. "What is it?"

"I just... thought I heard something."

He didn't look away. "Like what?"

She hesitated. "It's nothing. I'm just tired."

"I need to know what kind of 'nothing,' Lisa. You're my responsibility now."

She glanced away, her mouth dry. You already know, she thought. There was no point hiding it. "I heard a child laughing."

He was quiet for a long time. Then: "Alida?"

She froze.

Her eyes slowly met his. She hadn't expected him to say it. Not out loud. Not him.

"Yes," she whispered. "It was her."

"Is she following you?" he asked, tone unreadable.

"Following me?" She tried to sound light, but her voice cracked. "No. Of course not." The lie tasted bitter.

"Then why did you hear her?" he asked, gently but firmly.

She didn't answer. Because she couldn't. Because she didn't know. Because the laughter had sounded so real... so near.

"I feel like I'm going crazy," she finally muttered. "What's wrong with me?"

"There may not be anything wrong with you," he said. "There may be... other factors involved."

"What kind of factors?"

"That's all I'll say for now." He didn't elaborate. Instead, he reached forward and pressed the elevator button.

She watched him warily. "That's cryptic."

He gave a small smile. "I think you'll find I'm a man of many layers."

The elevator opened with a ding, and they rode it in silence. As the doors slid open on the first floor, he spoke again, more practical now. "Let's run by the store. Your new place is close to town. It's no trouble."

He wheeled her outside. The wind was cool and sharp against her face. She scanned the curb. Her cab was gone.

He led her to the staff lot, guiding her past the rows of dented sedans and rust-flecked compacts. His car was parked at the edge, a gleaming black Mercedes. She blinked at it, unsure why it surprised her.

Maybe it was just one more thing she didn't know anymore.

# CHAPTER 19

Koy had helped her transfer into the car with quiet ease, no fuss, no embarrassment, and returned the wheelchair himself without needing to ask a nurse. Doors seemed to open for him; red tape cut in his wake. Obviously, there were distinct advantages to being a physician.

Still, as she settled into the cool leather of the passenger seat, she couldn't shake the question: *Why* was he doing this? Not even her coworkers had offered to help. Not with a ride. Not with groceries. Not even a greeting card.

Maybe they didn't want to get involved. Grief made people uncomfortable. It reminded them how close it always was. But Koy?

She appreciated the sudden kindness, even if it left a thread of unease behind. He wasn't the type to blur lines. She couldn't accept the idea that he had any romantic or inappropriate interest in her. It didn't suit him. Not the man she'd known for over a decade. Not the physician who'd sat across from her and Hal countless times.

No. This felt different. Like maybe he sensed something coming, too. When he returned to the car, they pulled out of the parking lot in silence. The engine was quiet, the interior clean and sleek. She'd never ridden in a Mercedes before. In 33 years of life, it was a first.

He didn't speak until they'd left the hospital grounds and turned onto the highway. "Okay," he said, glancing at the road. "Now give me specific details about your hospital stay. In the elevator, you were listening to something. Is that all that's happened?"

She wanted to tell him about the nurse. About what she'd seen. About the figure that had lifted that poor woman into the air with its hair, the sobbing voice, the way everything blinked back to normal like it hadn't happened. She wanted to tell someone, needed to, but she hesitated.

"How much should I say?" she muttered, half to herself. Then louder: "First, I do not want my meds increased."

He nodded once. "If you don't want them increased, we won't increase them." A beat of silence passed. He didn't push. Then softly: "Is it that bad?"

She leaned back in the seat, carefully, painfully. "I don't know. I just know what I've seen. What I've felt. And it doesn't make sense."

He nodded again, waiting.

"And you don't believe in the supernatural?" she asked, glancing over at him.

He shrugged slightly. "I didn't say that. But I'm asking you... do you believe in it?"

"I don't... I didn't... I don't know what to believe anymore."

"Have you heard things more than once?"

"Yes."

"Seen things?"

"Yes."

"Then start from the beginning," he said. "From the very first day. Even if you think you've already told me something, tell me again. All of it."

They were on the highway now, the city slipping by in soft blurs of signage and stoplights. She felt something inside her give way, like a tight knot unspooling.

And she talked. Everything came out... the distant voices, the names whispered through closed doors, the sounds in the walls, the unnerving cold of the back bedroom, the door that never stayed shut. And finally, the nurse. The thing that lifted her, the flash of fury, the way it vanished like smoke.

She talked like she hadn't in weeks. Maybe months. Maybe since Hal died. He said nothing. Didn't interrupt once.

And for the first time, she didn't feel like a patient. She felt like someone heard. By the time she finished, her chest felt lighter. Exhausted, but lighter. She looked at him, expecting skepticism or concern. Maybe sympathy.

Instead, he just said, "There's something wrong with that bedroom."

The words hit her like a drop in temperature. Not comfort. Not relief. Fear. Because if he felt it, too. If someone else had sensed what she had... then it wasn't just her. It wasn't trauma, or grief, or the slow unspooling of a damaged mind. It was real. Real enough that someone else knew.

"That's where a lot of the noises seem to come from," she said quietly. "That room. I avoid it whenever I can."

"Have you checked the floorboards?"

She shook her head. "No. I haven't been able to do much of anything."

He didn't respond right away. His hands tightened slightly on the wheel. "I don't think it's tied to you," he said. "I think it's tied to the house. That room, specifically. Maybe even something, or someone, still there."

Her mouth went dry. "I don't understand why it's happening," she said, barely above a whisper.

"Neither do I," he replied. "But I'm going to help you find out."

# CHAPTER 20

"You need to call an exterminator first," Koy said matter-of-factly as they turned onto her street. "You need to make sure you don't have termites in your foundation. That should've been your first move when you bought the house. If there's any damage, it's better to know now... before it becomes catastrophic. And mice or rats can cause noises in the walls you'd swear were voices."

She nodded without answering. Of course she should've called an exterminator. Of course she should've had the house inspected. But logic had drowned weeks ago. She didn't bother adding if it was something she could afford. She didn't need to be reminded that she bought a cursed house with a grieving heart and a desperate budget.

They stopped at the store. Koy helped her into one of the electric customer scooters. She hated it. She hated how the seat gripped her hips. Hated the way it hummed beneath her. Hated the way people tried not to look at her but couldn't quite help it.

The bandages helped, gave them a reason not to stare too long, but humiliation clung to her like a second skin. By the time they returned to the car, her face was flushed with embarrassment. Koy returned the scooter without comment, and they rode the rest of the way in near silence, broken only by small talk and the occasional, awkward laughter.

Back at the house, he helped her inside, set the bags down, and, without asking, started a pot of coffee.

"You should drink more tea," he said as he poured two cups. "It's better for you."

"I know," she muttered.

But she didn't care. She wasn't interested in balance or antioxidants. She didn't exercise. Didn't count carbs. She didn't wake up early to meditate or drink smoothies or read labels to prolong her lifespan. She just wanted to survive each day without collapsing under the weight of loss. And if caffeine helped her do that, so be it.

"Can I see the room again?" he asked suddenly, setting his cup down.

"Go ahead," she said quickly. "I don't want to."

She stayed in the kitchen and sipped the bitter coffee. His footsteps moved down the hall. She saw rays of sunlight stream into the living room when he opened the back bedroom door. His shadow stretched across the opposite wall, long and strangely still.

And then... silence.

Too long.

"Koy?" she called. No answer.

Her stomach turned. She forced herself up and made her way down the hallway with careful steps, one hand gripping the wall. She reached the bedroom door and saw him standing there, frozen in place. His head was tilted upward. His eyes locked on the ceiling fan.

"Koy?" she said, trying to steady her voice. "Are you okay?"

He blinked. "What? Oh. Sorry. I was just... examining things."

She frowned. "What is it?"

"The fan," he said quietly. "It doesn't have the original blades."

"So?"

"It's odd. You can buy a new unit for the price of new blades. Why only replace the blades? And they're misaligned. Not mounted correctly. That's probably what's making the occasional noise."

"Okay, but is there anything else?"

He turned, walked slowly to the wall. "Where did you say you hit?"

She pointed. He ran his hand along the wall. Then he pulled a pencil from his shirt pocket and knocked on the drywall.

Dull thuds. Then a sharper one.

"This is an older wall. The drywall is compromised on the other side... probably water damage or age... but here?" He tapped again. "Completely intact. An impact that hard should've cracked the paint, at least. But it's solid."

"I felt it splinter when I hit," she said. "I heard it."

"I don't doubt you."

He stared at the wall, then looked at the ceiling again. "Do you mind if I check the fuse box?"

"It's in the basement."

She followed him as far as the top of the stairs. That was as far as her body would allow. He descended carefully. She heard the little metal door creak open, followed by the faint tapping of his pencil.

"Someone replaced the wiring," he called.

She turned back to the kitchen. She refilled her cup at the coffee pot.

Then: "Hello? Who are you?" Her head snapped up. The voice came from below.

"What is it?" she called down.

"A little blonde girl is outside. Is this Alida?"

Her throat tightened. "It must be."

"She's got a German shepherd with her?"

"That's Remus."

She heard the basement door open, hinges groaning in protest. The deadbolt clicked back. And then everything shifted. The atmosphere thickened. Her skin chilled.

A scream cut through the air, raw and female, eerily familiar. The dog growled. Something thudded. There was the sound of a scuffle, a heavy object colliding with something solid.

Then—slam. The outside door slammed shut. The bolt twisted. Footsteps. Fast. Rushing up the stairs. Koy burst into view, pale, shaking. He clutched his forearm. Blood seeped between his fingers.

"I locked the basement door," he panted. "Something's wrong."

She staggered back. "What happened? Did she run?"

"No," he said with a low voice. Shaken. He grabbed the dishtowel and wrapped it tightly around his arm.

"Lisa...." He gently placed both hands on her shoulders.

"This is not going to sound like a physician," he said. "So, prepare yourself."

She set her mug down, numb. Her eyes dropped to his arm. His forearm was bleeding... deep bite marks, raw and angry. "That little girl is not a little girl."

"What are you talking about?" she stammered. "The dog's protective. He barks, but he's not—"

"It wasn't the dog." Koy stepped past her, toward the sink His voice just above a whisper. "It wasn't the dog," he repeated. "The girl did this."

# CHAPTER 21

"Wasn't the dog?" she repeated, her voice barely above a whisper. She couldn't move, couldn't comprehend what he said.

"No." Koy removed the dishtowel and put his injury under the faucet. He turned the cold water on full blast and ran it over his arm, his jaw tight with pain.

"How badly are you hurt?" she asked. But when he pulled his arm from under the stream, her stomach turned.

"*She* bit me." Was all he said. It was worse than she imagined. His wrist looked mauled, like a raw, gory bracelet had been carved into his skin. A full circle of deep puncture wounds, as though two sets of canine jaws had clamped down from opposite sides. But that wasn't how bites worked. Not human, not animal. Bites didn't wrap around limbs. They couldn't curl in a full circle. It was like something had coiled around him.

"She...?" She blinked. "You can't be serious." Her tone was meant to sound incredulous, to inject a little humor into the surreal... but it fell flat. She didn't believe herself. Not really.

He didn't respond. He just turned his arm so she could see the wound clearly. Impossible. She felt her breath catch. "How many times were you bitten?"

"Once," he said.

She opened the cabinet under the sink, fumbled for the

first aid kit, but the pain in her back made it impossible to reach. He knelt down without a word and pulled it out himself.

She began pulling out the gauze and antiseptic as he dried his wrist, trying to think, to process. Her hands were mechanical, detached. "Should we talk to her parents?" she asked. "Find out what... who... she really is?"

He shook his head. "Parents? I don't think that thing has parents." The way he said *thing* chilled her.

"I don't know that talking to anyone will help," he added, voice tight. "It wouldn't matter. Not with something like that."

She watched him for a long moment. "You're not telling me everything."

It wasn't a question. She could see it in his eyes, the weight behind his silence. She'd told him everything: every hallucination, every whisper, every glimpse of a figure that vanished as soon as it appeared. He owed her more than vague warnings and cryptic hints.

"You should tell me," she said. "I have to live in this house. I'm the one who was attacked first. If something's happening, something real, I deserve to know what you suspect."

He sighed. His hands slowed. "It worries me, okay? That's why I haven't said more."

"What worries you?" she asked.

He didn't answer right away. And then she said something that hurt her as soon as it left her mouth: "When did this become our problem? You're not involved."

It wasn't fair. But she couldn't stop herself. She hated the look on his face when she said it, like she'd slapped him. "This is my house and my problem." She tried to soften her tone.

He finished wrapping the bandage around his arm. "You know that's not the whole story."

She folded her arms, suddenly cold.

"If I hadn't pushed you to move, none of this would've happened," he said. "I encouraged you. I thought I was helping. Now you're here, alone, and something in this place is... wrong."

"You didn't know," she said. "Neither of us did."

He shook his head. "I still feel responsible. Even more than you do. And I have to find a way to make it right."

He held her gaze. And for a long moment, she didn't say anything. Finally, she gave him a nod.

He stayed for a while longer, but neither of them spoke about the basement again. They tiptoed around it, spoke softly, and listened for the sound of laughter that never came.

The house felt heavier. Every corner, every hallway seemed darker than before. As if some unseen presence had grown more aware of them... had begun watching back.

She feared his leaving almost as much as she feared his staying. She couldn't afford to grow used to having someone in the home again. Not after Hal. Not when she knew Koy would have to leave, and she'd be left with nothing but shadows.

He downed the last of his second cup and stood, his movements slower than before. "I'm going to the courthouse," he said. "I want to dig into the house's history. There's something we're missing."

She nodded, though she felt her body tense. "You don't have to do that."

"I do, Lisa. I'm not okay leaving you here like this."

She smiled faintly, surprised by the warmth that flickered in her chest. "I'll be fine."

"You sure?"

"No. But what choice is there?"

He took a business card from his wallet and wrote on it. He handed it to her. "This is my cell number. If you hear anything, any sound, any whisper, anything that feels off, you get to your car, lock the doors, and call me. Immediately. Promise me."

"I promise."

He hesitated at the door. Then he left. And just like that, she was alone again.

She closed the door behind him and stood in the silence of her living room. It didn't feel like home. It never had. Not since the first night.

Why did Hal have to die? Why did he leave her to face this? She limped to the couch and lowered herself onto her stomach, careful with every motion.

She buried her face in her arm and whispered, "Just a nap. Just a little while."

But she didn't expect rest.

Not anymore.

# CHAPTER 22

She woke in a house that looked familiar. Not just familiar... known. But wrong. She'd been here before. She knew she had. Somewhere in the fog of memory, it existed. Not as a dream, but as a place. A place she'd once stood. Her house... but not.

The walls were the same shape, but nothing else matched. The flooring had transformed into a threadbare blue shag carpet that muffled every sound. The beige curtains she'd hung were now a ghostly white, too pristine, too still. The light filtering through the windows had that unreal, dreamlike quality, the kind of illumination that revealed everything but warmed nothing.

She moved through the living room with slow, deliberate steps. Her body still ached, though less than it should have. Pain was dulled, distant, like a warning behind thick glass.

A child screamed. Her stomach dropped. The cry came from the back of the house. The room. *The bad room.*

She forced herself down the hall. Her feet sank into the carpet like it was wet, and each step took too long. The door loomed at the end. Its frame darker than the others. She pushed it open.

Chaos erupted inside. A man, red-faced and shaking with fury, stomped across the room. He crushed every toy in his path, snapping plastic and shattering dreams beneath his boots. Crayons splintered underfoot like bones. He made a show of it, grinding each piece into the pink carpet.

Alida. Tiny and trembling, curled up in the corner like a discarded doll. Lisa's breath caught. The child sobbed into her knees; arms wrapped around her shins. Her pale curls were matted with tears. The man reached down, seized her by both arms, and shook.

She moved before thinking. "Stop it!" she shouted, but no one reacted. Her voice didn't exist here.

"You tell me what I should do with an ungrateful little

brat!" the man bellowed, spittle flying from his mouth.

A woman burst into the room behind her, ran through her. She gasped. The woman's long white-blond hair flew as she moved.

As it fell from her face, Lisa saw the bruises, dark, raw shadows bloomed under each eye like fingerprints. She tried to call out, to reach her, but the woman didn't see her. Didn't hear her.

This wasn't a dream. It was a memory.

The woman snatched Alida from the man's grasp and held her close. "Look what you did!" she cried. "Her arm! What if you broke it? I have to get it checked...."

"Oh, now you care?" His rage turned to scorn. "You're just gonna make up a story. Again. Lie like you always do."

"And if I don't?" She began to walk toward the door.

He grabbed her arm, hard, spun her back, nearly knocking Alida from her grasp. "You'll do it, bitch, or I'll kill both of you. You got that?"

Lisa stepped forward. Her fury rose even further. She grabbed the wooden chair from the child's desk, lifted it with all her strength, and swung it at his back.

It passed through him like mist. The chair never moved. It was still there, untouched, in its place. She stumbled back. Her breath hitched. It was too late. She couldn't help them now. They were beyond her.

The asshole stormed out, yelling curses into the hallway as he left the room. The woman sank onto the bed, holding her child close, rocking her gently. Alida wept into her shoulder.

"One day," the mother whispered, lips pressed to her daughter's head. "One day, we'll get away from him, baby. I promise."

She took a step closer. She could barely breathe. From the living room, the man's voice echoed: "I heard that! When hell freezes over. You try anything, anything, and you know what my family will do. Hell, I might just kill you myself. But sure, keep dreaming. You can look forward supervised visitation." The front door slammed.

Silence.

The little girl lifted her tear-streaked face. "What'll we do, Mama?"

Her mother didn't answer. She just kept rocking. "I don't know, baby," she whispered.

# CHAPTER 23

She gawked at them both, unabashed. She couldn't reconcile it, couldn't make sense of how the monster that had thrown her like a rag doll across the room was the same woman sitting here now, gently rocking her child on a unicorn-print comforter.

This... this trembling, bruised young mother, who murmured comfort into her daughter's hair, this was the thing from the bedroom? The figure with bleeding eyes and a throat ringed in bruises? This was her?

She sat carefully on the edge of the bed beside them. But the mattress didn't shift beneath her weight. The worn fabric didn't crease. The bed ignored her completely. She wasn't in that moment. She was beside it. Witness to it. She wept with them anyway. They couldn't hear her, and they wouldn't have understood. But she couldn't help herself.

"I'm so sorry," she whispered. "I'm sorry this happened to you." She wanted to hug them both. To shelter them from the monster in the living room. They were both just children. The mother couldn't have been older than her early 20s. They were both experiencing things that should not be. Ever.

The room had gone silent. No more yelling. No more threats from the other room. Just soft weeping, raw and exhausted, and two bodies holding on to each other as tightly as they could.

How could something so loving, so maternal, become that thing she'd seen? What turned her into the creature with blood-black eyes and rage that shattered the air? Was it death? Grief? Or something worse?

Soft padding reached the room. Remus trotted in, ears low, eyes alert. The giant shepherd whimpered once, then laid his massive head in the child's lap.

"See?" the woman said gently, stroking Alida's hair. "Remus is here now. He'll protect us. We won't let him out anymore."

She was trying to believe it. Lisa could hear it in her voice. This wasn't just reassurance for Alida, it was a desperate promise to herself. "We'll keep him right here."

Alida sniffled. "Where did Daddy go?"

"I don't know, baby," the woman said. Her voice dropped. "I don't care."

Then everything shifted. She felt herself falling, not physically, but as though the entire dream peeled away. She dropped through it, through the memory, through the floor. The room vanished. Blackness rushed in like water filling a sealed room.

A new sound replaced the silence. A low, metallic squeak, over and over. Something scraping, cyclical. Like a broken fan or a frayed belt grinding against itself. Then a faint groan. Maybe a cry. Or both.

Flickers of vision came in flashes, brief, like someone snapping photographs in the dark. A room. Strange. Unfamiliar.

Feet. Pale, female feet, dangling midair. They didn't move. Lisa stared. What were they doing up there? Were they climbing?

No. Not climbing. Hanging. A voice broke through the dark, as though from an old radio in the fog.

"The apparent murder-suicide was a shock to the Easton community and all those around..."

"The father is heartbroken and asks that everyone respect the family's privacy during this time of grieving..."

No. No, that man wasn't grieving. That wasn't heartbreak. She had seen him. The shouting, the violence, the threats.

Who were they talking about? If the father didn't do it... then who did? It couldn't have been Alida. Could it?

A woman's voice, distant, cried out from the void. "There's something here. Something that wants to tell us something... but what?"

Another voice, male, calm, slow. Southern. "I don't think

we need to continue this investigation when the answer is obvious. We know what happened that night..."

She tried to scream. To argue. To ask the questions no one wanted to answer. But then came a ringing. A sharp, shrill ringing, repetitive, mechanical, real.

She felt herself floating upward, rising out of the fog, the voices, the darkness. She blinked. Her eyes opened to dim daylight. She was on the couch. The phone. It was ringing. She reached for it, her hand fumbled with the receiver.

"Hello?"

The line crackled. A whisper, broken and trembling: "I'm sorry..."

She bolted upright, wincing as her muscles screamed in protest. "What? Who is this? What are you talking about?"

The whisper returned, more desperate now. "It's too late...." Then a choked sob. And the line went dead. A cold click followed by a monotonous busy signal. She stared at the receiver in her hand. Too late for what? She hung up and, on instinct, dialed the number trace code.

The robotic voice replied: "We're sorry, but the last number is not known."

Of course. Everyone was sorry. She was sorry her house was haunted. She was sorry she'd ever bought it. Sorry she listened when she should've trusted herself. Sorry Hal was gone. Sorry she'd been left behind to pick up the pieces. There was no shortage of sorry.

And there were no answers.

# CHAPTER 24

Drawn by a hunch she didn't fully understand, she stood and crossed to the side bedroom. To the small closet in the corner. The air felt heavier now. Not threatening. Just... watchful.

The closet had remained shut since she moved in. She hadn't wanted to deal with it, had barely looked inside. A stack of old boxes blocked the door, remnants of the previous owners that she'd meant to toss but hadn't gotten around to.

She hesitated for a moment, then pulled the door open. Dust swirled in the stale air. Most of the boxes inside were water-damaged and caved in.

She moved one aside and uncovered something flat wedged behind a bent shoe rack, something wrapped in an old manila folder, yellowed at the edges. She pulled it free. Inside were several papers. Utility bills. A lease agreement from 2010.

And then... the clipping.

She froze.

It was brittle, the newsprint thin and fragile. The headline was short, but it struck like a blow to the chest.

### "Tragedy on Easton Avenue: Mother and Daughter Dead in Suspected Murder-Suicide."

Bristol Herald Courier – September 2012

BRISTOL, VA – Authorities are investigating a suspected murder-suicide that occurred in a small home on Easton Avenue late Thursday night.

Police responded to the residence after a neighbor reported prolonged silence and an unusual odor coming from the property. Inside, officers discovered the bodies of 25-year-old Morgan Owen and her four-year-old daughter, Alida Owen.

Though officials have not released specific details about the cause of death, investigators confirmed that the scene showed "no signs of forced entry or outside involvement."

Morgan's husband and Alida's father, Mitchell Owen, was not present at the home and is not considered a suspect at this time. In a brief statement given to reporters Friday morning, Mr. Owen said: "This is a personal loss beyond words. I ask the public and the press to respect our privacy as we mourn."

Residents of the normally quiet neighborhood have expressed disbelief. One longtime neighbor, who requested not to be named, said, "I knew there were problems, but no one ever expected this."

The investigation remains ongoing. No further statements have been issued by the Bristol Police Department.

*Easton Avenue. Bristol, Virginia.* Her eyes scanned the article in a daze. Morgan Owen. Twenty-eight. Alida Owen. Four years old. She lowered herself onto the edge of the bed and kept reading, her mouth going dry.

The article mentioned a neighbor's call, an odor, the phrase "no signs of forced entry." Her breath hitched when she reached the quote from the husband, Mitchell:

> "This is a personal loss beyond words. I ask the public and the press to respect our privacy as we mourn."

Mourn? *Bullshit.* That man didn't mourn. He threatened. He raged. She had seen him. And now she knew. It wasn't just a dream. It wasn't just trauma bleeding into grief. Something happened in this house. And someone, maybe more than one, still wanted the truth to be told.

# CHAPTER 25

She heard it again... a rattling knock somewhere deep in the house. Not frantic, not constant. Just there, sporadic bursts of sound, like something trying to be discreet about being heard. Then silence.

The knocking returned, lasted about thirty seconds, and faded again. It repeated. Three times. Then a fourth. Each burst distinct. Almost like Morse code.

She froze, the open laptop sitting beside her on the couch, her hands hovering above the keys. She slowly closed it and set it aside.

The air in the house felt tighter now. Closer. She rose and moved carefully through the living room, listening to the rhythm of the sound. There was something behind it. Not just noise... intention.

The soft knocking became a low rumble. The kind of vibration you feel more than hear. It rolled through the floorboards like a distant drumbeat, steady and growing.

It was coming from the basement.

She stopped in the kitchen. Her hand resting lightly on the basement doorknob. *Don't go down there.* Her better judgment screamed it. *Whatever threw you across that bedroom is still here. Maybe waiting.*

She rested her head against the door, listening. The lock was still in place. The sound continued below, thud, pause, thud-thud, pause. It wasn't random. It was too measured. It wasn't the basement door. It sounded like a cardboard box.

She waited. Nothing else stirred. Her hand moved almost of its own accord, throwing the bolt. The door creaked open an inch. She leaned in, squinting down the stairs.

No child. No dog. Just a bare bulb casting dull yellow light. She reached in and flipped the switch. A long fluorescent tube flickered to life down below. The shadows retreated, but only a little. No movement. But the sound didn't stop.

She stepped onto the first stair. Then another. The wood creaked underfoot like it was holding its breath. The rumbling deepened the farther she descended. Not louder, just closer.

The bottom of the staircase opened into clutter and concrete. The air smelled like damp wood, dust, and something older, stale grief that lived in the walls. The sound was coming from the far-left corner.

A stack of old boxes trembled in place, as if something were trapped beneath them. She edged closer, each footstep feeling heavier than the last. Her spine itched with the pressure of being watched.

The boxes were plain, unlabeled. More remnants from the previous owners. She'd meant to sort through them but hadn't dared the stairs since her injury. Now she reached for the top two, carefully pushing them off the stack. They were surprisingly light.

The bottom box shook again. She hesitated, breath shallow. Then she peeled the top flaps open. Inside were old children's toys, scuffed dolls, broken crayons, plastic animals with paint rubbed off their eyes.

A dusty, beat-up camcorder sat on top. And just beneath it... She saw the hem of a unicorn-printed blanket. The same one from the bedroom in the vision. Her breath broke in her throat. Her knees buckled, and she caught herself against the wall. Tears welled up and spilled over before she could stop them.

*Oh my God.* Morgan and Alida lived here. They hadn't just died in this neighborhood. They died in *this house.* She was standing where it happened. Where it all ended.

She picked up the camera with trembling hands. The plastic was cold, too cold, and felt almost damp. The power light blinked red. Still charged. Still waiting. She didn't know what she would see.

Then... something moved at the edge of her vision. The narrow basement window set into the door. She turned. Alida stood outside. But it wasn't the sweet little girl who'd chased a ball through her yard. Not this time. Her eyes weren't human...

they were Remus's. Wide, glowing, too yellow. The pupils stretched too long.

And her mouth, that mouth, was wrong. It wasn't a child's smile. It was a muzzle. Canine. Split open with too many teeth. She pressed her face to the glass. And growled. A low, guttural growl, unmistakable. It rumbled through the windowpane and deep into Lisa's spine.

She stumbled back. She clutched the camcorder to her chest. The growl cut off as suddenly as it began. The girl was gone. Just the empty steps leading up to the backyard now. And a single pawprint, too large to be a dog's, fogged against the glass.

.

# CHAPTER 26

She hobbled up the stairs, one hand clutched the camera, the other dragged along the railing for support. Every step sent bolts of pain through her spine. Her back muscles throbbed like they were tearing open. By the time she reached the top, her breath came in short, shallow pulls.

She locked the basement door behind her and sagged against it. What was she doing? She wasn't a detective. She wasn't a ghost hunter. She was barely able to move without help. The idea of confronting whatever that thing was, whatever was out there growling behind a little girl's face, was insane. She wasn't equipped to fight it. But here she was.

The video camera in her hand was old, covered in wrinkled black electrical tape. Not haphazardly... deliberately. The lens, the recording light, even the control panel were all sealed. Like someone didn't want anyone to know it had ever been used.

She peeled the tape away, piece by tacky piece, until the buttons were visible again. Nothing seemed broken. The casing wasn't cracked. There was no reason for it to have been taped up at all. Which meant one thing: someone wanted to hide the fact it had been recording.

She plugged it into the television and sat in the recliner; one hand braced against the armrest to keep her posture steady. The camera whirred to life. And then Morgan. Her chest clenched. She looked exhausted, much more so than in the bedroom. Her face was swollen and mottled with bruises. Her lip was split and dried blood crusted at the corner of her mouth.

She stared into the camera. Her expression raw and vulnerable, like someone already halfway gone. "My name is Morgan Owen," she said, her voice trembling. "And I'm terrified."

She didn't breathe. "I decided to use this as a record of

what happens. Mitchell is coming home unexpectedly... I don't know why. He never does that. He's a long-haul driver. He shouldn't be back for another week."

Morgan paused. She pressed her fingers to her temple. A sob leaked out before she could stop it. "I'm afraid for Alida. If he kills me... who will take care of her? She's asleep now. I just hope she doesn't see anything. I'll delete this if I'm wrong, but I have a bad feeling...."

A crash offscreen. Morgan turned toward the sound. Seconds later, the front door slammed open. It sounded like it took half the wall with it.

"You simple-minded whore," a voice roared. Lisa's skin crawled. Him. "What did you do...?"

"What is it? I don't know..." Morgan's voice cracked.

"What the hell is this stain doing on my shirt? My favorite shirt. I've had it with your bullshit."

"Why don't you just leave?"

"And pay you child support?" He scoffed. "I don't even like the little bitch." A low growl rumbled in the background. Remus.

Morgan's body flew into the frame. He threw her into the coffee table. The wood splintered beneath her. She tried to crawl away, but he yanked the phone cord out of the wall.

"This ends tonight."

He wrapped the cord around her neck. Lisa's nails dug into the chair. Morgan struggled. Her fingers clawed at the wire. She couldn't get between it and her throat. She kicked. Her heels scraped against the floor. Her eyes bulged, her mouth opening and closing with no sound. Then... her body went limp.

He dragged her out of frame. A soft creaking began in the distance. The ceiling fan. She already knew which room it came from. Silence followed. Then: footsteps. Heavy. Unhurried. The camera remained still, forgotten.

He returned into frame. Carried a glass filled with something red. He set it directly in front of the lens. Her stomach turned. It wasn't wine. It was too red. It looked like strawberry Kool-Aid.

From his coat pocket, he pulled a packet of white

powder. He dumped it into the drink. Stirred it slowly.

"Alida?" he called, in a singsong voice. "I have a surprise for you." She gripped the arms of the chair until her knuckles whitened.

"Daddy?" A soft voice answered from the back.

"I brought you a strawberry drink... but you have to drink it all before it goes bad."

"You brought me a present?" Her voice lifted. Hopeful. Cautious.

"Yes. It'll help you sleep... better than ever."

Moments passed.

"Daddy? It tastes funny."

"It's supposed to, sweetheart."

She could see him in her mind, kneeling beside her bed with that plastic smile, feeding her poison as if it were a bedtime story. He walked back into frame a few minutes later and yanked the cord from the television.

"Remus," he called softly. The dog padded into the room. Sat. He knelt, whispered something. Scratched behind his ears. Then he slipped the cord over Remus's head. Yanked.

The dog crumpled instantly. She choked on a scream. She couldn't look away. He disappeared again, this time for longer. A muffled whimper came from Alida's room.

He came back with a pillow. It was over in seconds. He didn't even speak to her. When he returned, he looked directly into the camera for the first time. He didn't know it was recording.

He straightened his coat and said, "Goodbye... and good riddance." He went out the door. Strangely, the camera tumbled onto its side to film outside the front window. His shadow walked past the window and into the woods ahead. He must've parked several streets over.

She leaned forward, watching through the crooked view. Owen crossed the street in a dark hoodie and jeans, blending into the shadows. He ducked into a line of trees on the edge of the mountainside.

He never parked at the house. Never left a trace. She stared at the screen, heart thundering. Now she knew the truth.

And now... someone knew she knew.

# CHAPTER 27

*Murdered.* They were killed. She stared at the frozen image on the TV, then slowly turned her gaze back to the laptop screen. Her chest felt hollow, like her heart had retreated into some unreachable corner.

The camera had confirmed what her nightmares had only suggested. And now, the article staring back at her only sharpened the edges of it.

The second headline from the Bristol Herald Courier wasn't what she expected.

If anything, it made the first look tame.

### *FOLLOW-UP ON EASTON AVENUE TRAGEDY RAISES QUESTIONS*

October 3, 2012 – BRISTOL, VA

Just three weeks after the suspected murder-suicide that claimed the lives of Morgan Owen and her four-year-old daughter, Alida, new details have surfaced that cast doubt on the initial conclusion.

While authorities maintain that Morgan Owen acted alone in the deaths, unofficial sources within the department have expressed concern over several inconsistencies in the case files.

"There are things that don't line up," said one officer, who asked not to be named. "The timeline's off. Some of the physical evidence doesn't make sense. There were no fingerprints on the glass found beside the girl's bed, not even the mother's."

Additionally, autopsy results reportedly revealed inconsistencies in the manner of death. While initial reports stated that both mother and daughter died by asphyxiation, one forensic pathologist noted trauma that was "more consistent with strangulation from behind," which contradicts the official narrative.

The family dog, a German shepherd named Remus, was also found dead at the scene, but no necropsy was performed. According to the responding team, the animal's body was "disposed of off-record" due to decomposition.

> When asked for comment, Mitchell Owen, Morgan's husband and Alida's father, again stated he was "not home at the time," and that rumors suggesting otherwise were "reckless and disrespectful." He has not been charged with any crime.
>
> Despite this, the home at 147 Easton Avenue has remained vacant since the incident. A spokesperson for the realty company responsible for the listing said they've had "difficulty" reselling the property.
>
> "There's just... something about it," the rep admitted. "People walk in and walk right back out. We don't even finish showing it half the time."

She stopped reading. She sat very still. The glow from the screen lit the dark room in soft pulses. No fingerprints. Discrepancies in the time of death. Remus's body gone. The house had been a crime scene. And someone had buried the evidence.

Now, it wasn't just haunted. It was covered up. She scrolled down. There it was. A final statement issued months after the initial shock faded. Polished. Sanitized. Absolute.

> "After a lengthy investigation, the authorities conclude that the tragic events of the Easton community were the product of a murder-suicide.
>
> Authorities believe that Morgan Owen, knowing her husband was going to ask for a divorce when he returned, killed both the family's pet and her child, and then hung herself.
>
> This brings closure to a deeply painful moment in our city...."

*Closure.* She read it twice. Then again. They blamed Morgan. Not the man who'd torn open the door, screamed through the house, and snapped his child's dog's neck like it meant nothing. Not the man who'd poisoned a little girl and smiled while doing it. Not the man who'd walked calmly across the street and vanished into the trees.

They gave him privacy. They gave her the blame. *No wonder she is so angry.* She sat back, fists clenched in her lap, breath coming fast and shallow. The taste of copper rose in her mouth, like rage manifesting as blood.

They'd buried Morgan twice. First in the ground. Then under a lie. And someone in this town, maybe more than one person, helped.

The front door flew open and slammed against the wall. She yelped and stumbled backward. She saw a flash from the video she just watched.

Koy rushed in, breathless. His shirt stuck to him with sweat. His hair was windblown and eyes too wide. "We have to leave," he said. "Now."

"What?"

"I'm serious. We have to go."

"I know what's happening!" she blurted out. That stopped him cold.

"What?"

She hurried to the table, breath racing, words tumbling from her mouth. "The tape. The article. The video camera. Morgan recorded it... everything. Mitchell murdered them. It's all there."

He stepped forward and put a hand on her shoulder. "We need to make copies," he said, voice low. "And I know where we can go."

"I need to change. I, I can't..."

"Now, Lisa." His grip tightened. "We don't have time."

"I don't understand. What's the rush? We can fix this, Koy. We solved it."

"I have a bad feeling," he said, already moving toward the door. "Get your purse. Please."

She grabbed it, heart pounding. The urgency in his voice left no room for argument. She watched as he snatched the tape from the camera and double-checked the locks on the back door.

"What is it?" she asked. "Why now?" He didn't answer. He ushered her to the car, hands shaking as he unlocked it.

Inside, silence. The seatbelt clicked over her chest as he threw the car in reverse and peeled out of the driveway. They flew down the street, past silent houses, past the rows of dull, watching windows.

"I don't understand," she said again. "It's okay now. We

know. They just want justice, Koy."

"We don't know, Lisa," he muttered, turning sharply onto another street. "Don't place all your hope on that."

"But it's Morgan and Alida. It's them. They just wanted someone to believe them."

"Maybe," he said tightly. "Or maybe not."

"What?"

"I wasn't attacked for attention," he said, eyes locked on the road. "That thing in the basement wasn't trying to explain itself. It was trying to break me."

She swallowed hard.

"Sometimes there are bad spirits," he continued. "You can call them ghosts, demons, whatever you want. But they're not misunderstood. They're malicious. They don't want peace. They want to hurt."

"But that little girl..." she started.

"May not be a little girl at all," he interrupted. "Whatever you saw... it might just wear their faces."

She turned to him slowly. Her mind fought it. Her heart rebelled. But something cold was settling into her gut.

"Even if it does stop," he said, "even if everything just... ends, you need to find a new home. I'll help."

"Why?" she whispered.

"Because I rushed you," he said. "I pushed you to move. I told you it would help. I put you there." He hesitated. "And because I care. As your physician... and as your friend."

She looked at him, at the tight line in his jaw. The sweat still clinging to his forehead. He meant it. "I have a guest house," he said. "It's yours until you find something else."

She stared out the window. The houses blurred past. The trees looked darker now, even under daylight.

"It's just a spirit," she said softly. "It's not like it's... following us."

"What if it does?" he said. "What if it's not done with you?" She said nothing. "What if it had snapped your neck instead of just bruising your back?"

The words cut deeper than she expected. She remembered that video, the cord, the sound, the body slumping.

Her stomach turned. "Where are you going with all this?" she asked.

"I think this thing," he said, "whatever it is... it's not just a ghost. It's not Morgan. It's not Alida."

"Then who is it?"

He looked at her. His voice dropped to a whisper. "I think something came in the moment Mitchell Owen did what he did."

She turned to him, wide-eyed. "Murdering your spouse in a jealous rage is one thing," Koy said. "But killing your child? Poisoning her? Killing the family dog with your hands?" He shook his head. "That kind of evil doesn't just vanish. It invites something."

She didn't argue. She couldn't. The facts were already twisting, already warping into something far worse than any haunting. She wanted to believe it was just a tragic story desperate to be heard.

But now? Now she wasn't sure who was haunting the house... or who was using it to get in.

# CHAPTER 28

Maybe it was more than just restless spirits looking for peace. She wasn't ready to admit that yet. But deep down, something in her bones told her Koy was right. Something wasn't done with her yet.

She leaned back against the passenger seat and let her head rest. The pain in her back throbbed with every bump in the road. Still, she felt lighter just not being inside that house. It wasn't much, but it was something.

At least Koy was driving. She was already so sick of driving. They pulled into a strange little strip mall on the far side of town. It was older, faded signage, low windows, cracked asphalt. She never would have guessed it was still in business. There was an archaic tech store at the end. Ancient posters of old VCRs, film cameras, and VCR tapes were in several windows.

"This is my uncle's shop," he said as he parked in front of the small storefront. Several small posters on the door had Japanese lettering and a picture of an old-school camcorder. "He has a machine that can make copies of the tape in a fraction of the time it would take me to do it."

They stepped inside. The walls were lined with boxes, film canisters, and stacks of electronics in various stages of usefulness. The shop smelled faintly of solder and aging plastic.

He greeted the man behind the counter in rapid Japanese. The two exchanged a flurry of words... clipped, respectful, familiar.

"This is my uncle, Sohiko," Koy explained. "I told him about your injury. He has trouble with English, so don't be offended if he's quiet." Sohiko gave a polite bow and gently shook her hand. His grip was surprisingly warm.

Koy handed him the camera tape. "I asked for five copies, for now. I'll keep one. You should hold on to the original. The rest will go to the state police, along with printouts of the articles. I already have everything queued to print."

She nodded, though her stomach turned just thinking about watching the footage again. "How do I explain how I found it?" she asked.

"Just the truth. You were cleaning out the basement, going through boxes the last owners left behind, and found the camcorder. That's all you have to say."

They followed Sohiko to a small room off the side of the shop. A low couch, a small table, and an old TV filled the space. The air hummed quietly from a ceiling fan.

They watched as the video started playing again. The footage was just as horrific the second time. She stared at Morgan's broken face on screen and felt the weight of that house settling back on her chest. She quickly wiped away the tears that slowly came.

"I don't understand something," she whispered to Koy.

He turned.

She kept her voice low. "Who turned the camera on its side?"

Koy hesitated. "We don't know. Maybe the wind. Maybe the spirits were already stirred up."

Or maybe someone else had been in that house that night. Something no longer human.

Koy and Sohiko exchanged more words in Japanese. She did her best to look distracted. She shifted her focus to a bright-red calendar pinned to the wall, or the thick newspaper folded beside her. The characters were beautiful, even if she couldn't read them. Their shapes looked ancient.

After a few minutes, he turned back to her. "Uncle said you shouldn't go back to the house for any reason."

"I have to," she said quietly. "I don't have anywhere else."

Koy shook his head. "I don't know how you get rid of something like this. Whatever damage was done in that house... it happened years ago."

"What about an exorcism?"

"An exorcism?" He blinked, then translated the term for his uncle. A brief, rapid exchange followed.

"I haven't been to church since Hal's funeral," she admitted, eyes cast down. "I wouldn't even know who to ask."

"It's not always a minister," Koy said. "There are other professionals dedicated to it. Uncle knows someone."

Sohiko suddenly grinned and held up a yellowing sheet of paper. The text was written in vertical columns, archaic Japanese characters, almost brush-like in their style. Koy opened his phone, made a call, and stepped into the hallway.

Sohiko turned back to her. "You... speak only English?"

"Yes." She smiled back. "Sorry."

"You have bad spirit in house," he said softly. "It not leave."

"Yes."

"You take care. Is difficult life." There was something comforting in his words. The way he said them wasn't pitiful. It was kind. Compassionate. And somehow, resigned.

"I don't know much about spirits." She looked down at her hands.

"Spirits everywhere." He gestured slowly, raising both hands. "All around. We no see... don't mean they gone."

"This one is very bad."

"You have... hungry ghost."

She frowned. "What's that?"

He thought for a moment. "Ghost has hunger. Always want more. Come from famine... want... murder." His voice lowered. "Back home, people live hard life. Die poor. Angry. Come back hungry."

"Yes," she said, surprised by the tears pricking her eyes. "That's it. That's what it feels like."

"You must leave. House belong to spirit now. You can't make it full. It always want more."

The machine beside them beeped. The fourth copy was done. The fifth had started.

He was probably right. Maybe the spirit at the house wasn't Morgan. Maybe it wasn't even Alida. Maybe it was what they'd left behind. Maybe Owen's cruelty had birthed something that couldn't be named.

Maybe the abused had become the abuser. Maybe they were trapped in that cycle, repeating it over and over. Koy returned. His tone was steady, but his face looked a little pale.

"I found someone," he said. "He calls himself an Appalachian exorcist. He practices traditional Appalachian Christian rites. I convinced him to meet us. He'll be at the house in two hours."

She blinked. "That's a thing?"

"It is," Koy said. "They're hard to find. They don't advertise."

"I spoke with your uncle a little bit."

"Yes, he's very quiet at first, but if you give him time, he'll open up." He accepted the final batch of tapes from Sohiko, then looked back at her. "He made seven. Not five."

"Overkill?"

"I don't trust the mail. This way, a few can go out today, a few can go later. Redundancy is good when you're talking about evidence of murder."

They exchanged goodbyes and walked back out into the parking lot. The wind had picked up a little. Koy held the door open as she climbed in.

As they drove to the post office, Lisa watched the clouds above, gray and disheveled, but softening. A few faint bands of blue broke through. She hadn't seen blue sky in days.

She leaned back and let her eyes close. Maybe, just maybe, it wasn't all death. Maybe it wasn't just about grief. Maybe there was something left in the world to look forward to.

# CHAPTER 29

They came to a stop in the drive and let the engine tick quietly beneath the sudden stillness. Koy stepped out, walked around, and opened the door for her. She hesitated. She wasn't ready. But she had to go in. There was no avoiding it now.

The front door creaked open under his hand. "I know I locked that," Koy muttered, low and wary. "Stay behind me."

The house was still. They moved cautiously from room to room. Nothing was missing. Nothing looked ransacked.

"It might be dangerous to walk into a robbery," he said, glancing around, "but... apparently nobody touches this house. Even with the door open, no one came. They know."

The kitchen was the same. The back door was standing open, curtains fluttering like breath. She closed it.

"What should I get?" she asked, voice dry.

"Clothes. Toiletries. What you need for now. We'll come back for the rest later. I doubt anyone's in a hurry to take your things."

Her instinct was to refuse help. She wanted to stand on her own, always had. After Hal died, that need doubled. She didn't want to owe anyone, and she sure as hell didn't want pity. But fear had a way of thinning the walls she'd built. And she didn't want to be alone in that house another night.

Her body protested with every step. She packed slowly, painfully, dragging her injuries along with the weight of everything else. Two bags. That's all she could manage.

Then came a knock at the door.

"I'll get it," he called from the living room. She listened to the voices. Male. Calm.

A moment later, Koy returned with a man at his side,

tall, rail-thin, dressed in black jeans and a long overcoat. His hair was white, wild, and his beard was a mountain in its own right. But it was his eyes that struck her still, icy blue, glinting with something ancient.

"This is Cecil Clark," Koy said. "He's the exorcist."

Lisa swallowed. "Do you know what's wrong with my house?"

Cecil didn't blink. "It's possessed. I could feel it down the street. It's a bad one, too." He said it like someone commenting on the weather. Flat. Final.

"You deal with that often?"

"Every week."

"What do I do?" She felt absolutely ignorant. She had no idea of what to do or how to do it.

"You'll help me. Then you'll leave for a few days. Cleanse your mind. The house can be cleansed, but trauma lingers. Fear does more damage than spirits ever could."

Her voice cracked. "So, I can keep the house?"

"You can," he nodded. "But I don't recommend it. Fear doesn't care how brave you are. It stays in your bones, even when your mind says everything's fine. The strongest memory always wins. And this place... it doesn't forget easy."

He cleared his throat and opened his Bible. He began reciting various passages. Then all hell broke loose.

The walls trembled. Pictures tore from their nails and shattered against the hardwood. A grotesque, black-red sludge seeped from the corners of the ceiling, dripping like infected wounds. Chunks of drywall exploded above them, raining powder. The air groaned. The house groaned.

Cecil didn't flinch. Even as parts of the house flew by his head. He dusted the debris from his bible and continued. He recited scripture with a steady, rising rhythm. His voice cut through the chaos like a blade through silk.

She clung to the hallway arch as the lights flickered. In the kitchen, plates hit the floor. She heard her grandmother's china smash.

"Koy!" she gasped.

He was beside her, tense. "It's trying to stop him. He's a

threat to it."

The basement wailed. Cecil passed her the Bible and motioned for them to read. She followed his lead. Their voices joined his.

The house hated it. She realized that what they dealt with was not just a murdered mother and child. Whatever it was raged against their attempt.

The floor bucked. The ceiling cracked deeper. The sludge crawled down the walls like vines of rot. Something inhuman screamed. Then, suddenly, it was quiet.

Not calm. Not settled. Silent.

"It's gone," Cecil said, soaked in sweat. He leaned on the entryway, breathing hard. "It's over."

She stared around her. The house had... healed. The walls were clean. The ceiling was whole. The television stood undisturbed on its stand.

She stepped into the kitchen. The dishes, whole. The stove, straight. The sink, dry. Everything was intact. Not even a fingerprint out of place. She put a hand on Koy's shoulder for balance. Her legs wobbled.

"Koy," she whispered. "It's really gone."

He nodded. He didn't smile. He just kept watching, like it might all revert if he blinked.

Cecil needed rest. They let him be. She moved from room to room. The air was different now. No more weight. No more pressure on her chest.

But there was one door left.

She stepped into the hallway. The bedroom. The bad room. She opened the door and stopped breathing. There were no walls. No floor. Just grass. Soft as velvet. Bright and sunlit.

Tall emerald hedges bordered either side of her, perfectly trimmed. White roses bloomed everywhere, untouched by thorns or insects. In the distance, a marble temple stood with towering Greek columns, like Delphi itself. It was exquisite.

Then laughter, soft, pure, broke the silence. She held her breath again. Morgan ran toward her in a white silk dress, her hair shining gold. She looked like something pulled from myth, radiant, joyful, whole. "Thank you," she whispered, and hugged her. Warm arms. A real embrace.

Her voice. It had been her voice, Lisa realized. Whispering her name the day she moved in. Then came Alida, her tiny feet light in the grass. Her beautiful dress matched her mother's. Her hair was braided into a crown. They looked like mythic queen and her beautiful princess.

Remus followed close behind, tail wagging. Morgan picked Alida up and kissed her cheek.

"We're free," she said, tears in her eyes. "We're free."

Lisa smiled, soft, small, real. And for the first time in what felt like a lifetime, her own heart whispered something back. *So am I.*

# CHAPTER 30

As quick as breath, the vision vanished. The hedges. The white roses. The marble columns. Gone.

No courtyard. No ethereal garden. Just a plain, square room that had nearly broken her body and spirit.

The old beige carpet was back, threadbare and tired, but the weight was gone. The suffocating pressure that used to cling to the walls like mold had lifted. The room was just a room now. It wasn't watching. It wasn't remembering.

She turned. The door behind her was closed. And on the back, drawn in crayon, were looping, uneven letters:

"Thank you."

Beneath it, a child's drawing: a field of white flowers. A small girl in pigtails holding the leash of a floppy-eared dog. A woman in a white dress beside them, smiling.

She stared at it. Her chest tightened, but not with fear. She reached out and touched the waxy lines. They were still warm. She didn't speak. There wasn't anything left to say. She left the room, her steps slower now. Measured.

In the living room, Cecil stood by the door. He looked tired, but strong, like someone who had just lifted something too heavy, and set it down for good. She stopped in front of him, unsure of what to say.

"What did you do?" she finally asked.

He gave a small smile. "You can feel it, can't you?"

She nodded. "It's... clean."

He returned her hug gently when she stepped forward, then pulled back with a quiet chuckle. "That's why I do this," he said. "That feeling right there."

"Where did it go?" she asked him, voice soft.

"The same place it came from," he said.

She wanted to believe that meant it was gone forever. That they were finally at peace. That no one else would suffer here again. "Will it stay gone?" she asked.

"Yes," Cecil said, quieter now. "It's finished."

Lisa looked around. The air felt lighter. The walls didn't press in. The house wasn't haunted anymore. But she still was.

The memory of the screams, of the shadow in the hall, of the pain, those would linger far longer than the spirits had. The house might have been cleansed, but she had been changed.

She knew then that she couldn't stay. Not in these walls. Not with the echo of everything that had happened. She turned to Koy.

"I think I need a new start... again." she said.

He nodded like he'd been waiting for her to say it. He smiled. "I'll help you find it."

This wasn't her house anymore. It had never really been. It belonged to Morgan and Alida. Their chapter was closed, but hers wasn't.

She stepped outside into the late afternoon sun, her breath steady. For the first time in a long time, the world didn't feel like it was closing in.

It felt like it was opening up.

# Chapter 31

Koy didn't go home.

He dropped Lisa at the guesthouse with a promise to return by evening. He turned his car toward the city center, the hospital badge still clipped to his jacket. It got him in doors. More importantly, it bought him trust.

He didn't know what exactly he was looking for, just that something about the way Lisa described her encounter, and how the house felt when he was inside it, didn't sit right. He didn't just want to turn the tape into the authorities. There was too much potential for accidents or interference.

He knew trauma. He'd studied it, treated it, watched it hollow people out. But the fear in Lisa hadn't been a response to grief or psychosis. It had been real. Rooted. And old.

He started with the records office at the Bristol Police Department. He'd expected a brief search and a few open documents. What he got was an icy stare from the woman behind the glass and a clipboard of forms. "Owen?" she asked. "That case is closed."

"I'm aware," Koy said. "But I'm doing a private wellness evaluation on a new patient and need the original incident report. There are concerns... patterns we'd like to confirm."

The woman frowned, fingers tapping her keyboard. "You'll need to go through the public records request process. Processing times are three to five weeks."

He didn't argue. He made the request. And then he left. The next stop was the elementary school.

The principal who'd been there during the Owen incident was now retired, but he spoke with her replacement. The woman wore a pleasant expression that never quite reached her eyes.

"There were concerns at the time," she admitted. "But I wasn't working here yet. All I can say is... some of the staff expressed regret over how things were handled."

"Regret?"

"There was talk. Some of the teachers tried to escalate concerns about Alida. But when they finally saw injuries on her mother as well, the assumption was that Morgan was unstable."

He stared at her. "You mean they thought she was hurting herself?"

The woman shifted. "I'm not saying that's what happened. Just that there were rumors. Whispers. A lot of assumptions made... based on not very much."

"And no one followed up?"

The principal's face hardened slightly. "Mr. Owen's family had a lot of influence. They donated a new computer lab the year before. They hosted fundraisers. People felt... conflicted." He left with a pressure in his chest that had nothing to do with the cold.

At the social services building, the air was heavier. He didn't get past the front desk. The intake clerk, a heavyset man in his fifties with reading glasses, recognized the name immediately.

"That file's sealed," he said flatly.

"Why?" Koy asked.

"Because the child is deceased. Because the parents are deceased. Because the case was ruled a murder-suicide and there are no surviving parties with custodial interest."

He didn't bother hiding his frustration. "So, no one thought to question why a child's bruises kept matching her mother's? Or why neither of them were seen for days before the bodies were found?"

The man lowered his voice. "Look. Off the record? I remember the intake. The CPS worker flagged it. There were concerns. But the system's overloaded. When someone with the Owen name says it's all under control, most people back off."

"But not everyone," Koy said.

"No. Not everyone."

Back in his car, Koy sat in silence for a long time. The weight of what he'd learned settled deep into his ribs. Lisa hadn't just stumbled into a haunted house. She'd walked straight into the forgotten truth of a town too proud, too lazy, or too afraid to face what had happened.

The authorities didn't ask the right questions because they didn't want the answers. The system didn't protect Morgan or Alida. They buried them twice, once in the ground, and again in paperwork. The house remembered. And now it wanted someone else to. He turned the key in the ignition and drove back toward Lisa. He had work to do.

# Chapter 32

He called to check on Lisa, but she was fine. She was going to take a nap. He didn't tell her what he'd learned. Not yet. She sounded more relaxed than she had since Hal died. She needed space to breathe. To recover. He investigated alone and preferred it that way. The courthouse was next.

He wasn't expecting much. He just wanted to review the property records, confirm who had owned the house, whether there'd ever been other complaints, lawsuits, anything to explain why such a structurally questionable home had been passed off as livable. Lisa would never heal in that house. Even if it were quiet. He counted a dozen health hazards, just in a cursory walk-through.

The clerk was polite. Too polite. "147 Easton?" she asked, eyes flicking up from her screen. "You're not the first person to ask about that one."

"Really? Who else?" Koy asked.

"State legal rep. Someone from the DA's office. Couple of journalists."

"Recently?"

"Last few months."

Koy frowned. "And what were they looking for?"

"Same as you. Ownership history. Occupancy timeline. Public complaints." She tapped her nails on the desk. "Only thing is, all the documents you want are flagged."

"Flagged?"

"Marked private. Judge's order."

"Why?"

"'Family interest.'" She smirked bitterly. "You know what that means."

The Owen family had connections in half the county. That phrase, *family interest*, was the same used to close off estate records, death certificates, sealed testimony.

A wall of silence. But it didn't stop him. He reached out to a local reporter next, Samantha Kline, one of the only names he could find associated with a story on the case.

They met at a diner just off the interstate. She was sharp-eyed, no-nonsense, mid-thirties. Her notepad was already open when he arrived. "I figured someone would come knocking," she said, stirring cream into her coffee. "I didn't expect it to be a doctor."

"I'm a friend of Lisa's."

"You mean the woman who lived in that house after the murders?"

He nodded. She leaned forward. "Then you know the story's not over."

"What happened back then?" Koy asked.

She tilted her head. "What do you think happened?"

"I think Mitchell Owen murdered his wife, his daughter, and their dog. I think the police ignored red flags. And I think the family used their money and name to keep everyone quiet."

"Then we're on the same page."

Koy leaned in. "Why didn't you run the real story?"

She tapped her pen against the table. "Because I didn't have enough. The family's lawyers threatened to sue the paper. They said we were slandering a grieving father. My editor killed the piece. Buried it."

"You believed Owen did it?"

"I knew he did it. But back then, it was just a hunch. A timeline that didn't make sense. A series of bruises that no one documented. A police report that read like a press release. No camera. No footage. Just my word against theirs." She paused. "Until now."

He sat back in his seat. The waitress poured more coffee. The smell of burned bacon lingered in the air.

"Where do I start?" he asked her.

Samantha slid a folded piece of paper across the table. "Start with the detective who first arrived at the house. Joseph Cray. He quit six weeks later. No one ever asked why."

# Chapter 33

Joseph Cray didn't live in Bristol anymore. He'd retired to a small, worn-down cabin outside Lebanon, Virginia. Samantha gave Koy the address, along with a warning.

"He won't talk to just anyone," she said. "But if he answers the door, be patient. And don't lie. He hates that."

The cabin was barely visible from the road... shielded by trees that hadn't seen a trimmer in years. He parked beside a rusty pickup truck and walked the gravel path. The porch sagged at one corner. A windchime made from silver keys rattled with every breeze.

He knocked once. Then again. Finally, the door creaked open a few inches.

Cray stood behind the screen, unshaven, eyes heavy and lined. He looked older than Koy expected. Mid-fifties, maybe. But worn thin.

"You're not with the department," he said flatly.

"No, sir."

"You a lawyer?"

"No. Physician. Friend of Lisa Tillman."

The name gave him pause. "You mean the woman who moved into that house?" His voice dropped. "The Easton house?"

"Yes."

"Come in." Cray opened the door. No questions. No hesitation. The inside smelled like wood and old paper. Cray didn't offer coffee. Didn't sit.

"What do you want to know?"

He kept his voice level. "I want to know why you left the department."

Cray gave a humorless laugh. "That's the question, isn't it?"

He walked to a cluttered bookshelf and pulled down a dusty accordion folder. He dropped it on the table. Loose papers, faded photos, and two cassette tapes slid across the wood.

"I've been waiting for someone to come back around," he said. "I figured it'd be a reporter, or maybe one of the Owen lawyers sniffing for leverage."

"What happened, Detective?"

He didn't answer right away. Instead, he opened the folder and held up a picture. It was of Morgan Owen.

Her face was bruised, badly, but she was smiling. A school event, maybe. A paper badge pinned to her dress read "FIELD DAY – 2012."

"She brought that in herself," Cray said. "A week before she died. Said she needed to document something. She wanted it on record. She gave us pictures, copies of emails, even an old voicemail from Mitchell threatening her. I filed it all. I did my job." He looked up at Koy, eyes glassy. "Then it disappeared."

"What do you mean?"

"I mean it was gone the next day. Every file. Every photo. Her statements, my report, all of it. Wiped. My captain told me the family wanted to 'avoid embarrassment.' Said it was a domestic misunderstanding. That Morgan was mentally unstable."

"She wasn't."

"No," Cray said. "She was scared. But she was trying."

He paused. "I found the photos later. In a drawer in Records. Misfiled under a wrong case number. A coincidence, they said. Just a mix-up."

"And the autopsy?"

Cray's jaw tightened. "They sealed it fast. Didn't share the report with the full team. Just said it matched the story. Mitchell's version. Suicide. Murder-suicide, if you believed the spin."

"But you didn't."

"No. And neither did a few others. But they made it clear, drop it, or transfer."

"So, you resigned."

"Yep."

Cray looked at Koy, his expression unreadable. "But I kept copies. Not all, but enough."

He slid one of the cassette tapes forward.

"This is the audio from the night I arrived. Body cams weren't standard then, but I used a personal recorder for liability."

"May I?"

"Take it. Use it."

He pocketed the tape. "Why are you helping me?" he asked quietly.

Cray finally sat, slow and tired. "Because you're the first one who's asked the right question. And maybe because I've seen things I can't explain. And I think whatever happened in that house... isn't finished yet."

# Chapter 34

Koy sat alone in his study that night. The room was quiet, heavy with tension. He locked the door out of instinct, even though no one was expected.

He slid the cassette into his old tape deck. The wheels whirred to life with a faint static hum. Then—click.

A burst of wind. The car door closed.

"8:47 PM," Cray's voice said, calm but clipped. "Arriving on site. Owen residence. Dispatch flagged it after an anonymous call reported a foul odor and no movement in several days."

The sound of boots crunching gravel. A knock. Then another. "Police. Open the door."

A long silence followed. Static hissed in the background. "Front door's unlocked. Entering residence."

The door creaked open. Then silence. No voices. No footsteps. Just breathing. Heavy and uneven.

Cray whispered into the recorder. "Smells like copper. Heavy. Like rust."

He moved farther in. A clatter. Something metal fell. Then, "Oh... God."

The breath caught in Koy's throat. Cray's voice shook, barely audible. "There's a body. Female. Hanging from a ceiling fan. Visible bruising. Ligature mark at neck consistent with cord. Appears postmortem."

He paused, then: "Another body... child. Pale. Lips blue. Eyes half open. No visible wounds. No trauma. Pillow beside her head soaked through. No movement. Oh God, the dog's in the kitchen. Same signs. Rigor."

Koy leaned forward. The air on the tape had changed. There was something in it, some kind of hum underneath the silence.

Then Cray's voice dropped again. He sounded far away

from the mic now. "This wasn't just a domestic gone wrong. Something's... wrong with the house. I swear I heard something whispering in the hallway. No windows open."

More shuffling. Then a long silence. Whispers. Not Cray. Not intelligible. But not mechanical. Human, just at the edge of hearing. Dozens of them layered on top of each other. Crying, laughing, murmuring.

A thud.

Then Cray's voice again, sharper now, scared. "Door slammed behind me. Nobody here. Lights flickering. I'm exiting. I repeat, I am exiting the premises. This place is wrong."

The tape clicked and stopped. Koy stared at the deck for a long time. He rewound it. He didn't need to listen again. Not yet. He just sat there, in the dark, and tried to breathe. The tape confirmed it, something happened in that house beyond death. Beyond logic. Something layered into the very bones of it. Cray heard it too. Felt it. And he walked away.

Now Koy had walked in. And he wasn't sure they could walk out again.

# Chapter 32

Koy drove to his uncle's house in silence. Cray's cassette sat on the passenger seat like it might bite. It hadn't left his sight since he played it. Not in the car. Not in the house. Some things, once heard, never leave. He couldn't forget Cray's voice any more than he could Morgan's. She still haunted him.

Sohiko lived in a modest home near the edge of town, tucked behind a curtain of pines. The garden out front was wild but intentional, lavender and mugwort, thyme and white sage. All things that meant something once, even if the modern world forgot.

He knocked only once. The door opened before the knock finished echoing.

"Boy," his grandfather said, eyes narrowing. "You brought something dark."

Koy nodded. "I need your help."

Sohiko didn't ask for details. He stepped aside, then motioned to the low table in the center of the sunroom. The same table where Koy had once sat at age seven, terrified after a nightmare, and watched his uncle draw chalk sigils in the dirt.

They sat cross-legged. Koy handed over the tape. Sohiko didn't put it in the deck yet. First, he lit a stick of sandalwood incense and placed it upright in a black clay bowl next to the player. Only then did he insert it.

They listened. Cray's voice. The sounds. The whispering. And then, the slam. The humming. The voices no one could trace. Sohiko didn't flinch. But his hand clenched once on his knee. When it ended, he sat in silence, letting the tape click to a stop.

Koy finally broke it. "What is it?"

Uncle spoke slowly, not in English.

Koy waited until he switched back.

"That house holds more than memory," Sohiko said. "It

has absorbed something. A wrong act done in the presence of deep emotion, fear, betrayal, violence, can open a space. A gap. And if the soul doesn't cross over, something else moves in."

"A ghost?"

"No. Not the woman. Not the child. Not the dog." He looked up. "What stayed behind was born from it. Fed by it. The pain became its own thing."

Koy frowned. "Something like a... tulpa?"

"No. Tulpas are willed into being. This... this is more like a parasite. A spiritual wasp nest. A hungry ghost, yes. But also something more primal."

"Can it be destroyed?"

Sohiko shook his head. "Not destroyed. Starved. Displaced. That man who helped you, Cecil Clark, he did more than just speak prayers. He sealed the doors. Gave the house a new spiritual anchor."

"I thought as much."

"He's the reason you're both alive. But mark this..." Sohiko 's tone turned sharp. "You cannot unring the bell. Lisa's home saw the worst of human nature. And something saw her back. That's not something that goes away. Not really."

Koy leaned back, the cassette clicking in its deck again as if confirming the words.

"Do you think the police knew?" he asked.

Sohiko nodded slowly. "They knew something was wrong. But fear makes men do strange things. Easier to blame a woman no longer alive than face what they couldn't explain."

Koy exhaled. "Then what now?"

"Now, you keep Lisa away from that place. And you never listen to that tape again. Copy it. Store it. But don't invite it back in."

Koy stared at the deck. The incense burned low beside them. And through the open window, a wind stirred the pine branches like a warning whispered in a language only the bones remembered.

# Chapter 33

Koy didn't sleep that night. He still hadn't told Lisa everything. Partly because she still seemed weak, but partly because he wanted peace for all of them. He was as drawn into it now as Lisa. It was his fault they were all in that situation. He pushed Lisa too hard. She wasn't anywhere near ready to make those decisions.

He returned to his house and made another two copies of the tape. One he buried in his filing cabinet under a stack of insurance records no one ever asked for. The other he mailed, unsigned, to a retired investigator he trusted from his internship years ago. Just in case.

Then, he turned his attention to the Owen name.

There weren't many of them in the area. Mitchell's family, the old money types from northeast Virginia, had withdrawn completely from public view after Mogan died. His parents had shuttered their home.

Koy started there.

Alan Owens, Mitchell's older by four years, had once been in the news himself, for founding a biotech company that went public and flopped. After that, he'd disappeared. Now, he worked quietly at a small university research facility in Roanoke.

He didn't bother with subterfuge. He called, gave his name, said it was regarding Mitchell.

Alan agreed to meet. "But not at the lab," he added. "And not on the record."

They met at a tiny diner near the edge of town, white booths, sticky sugar jars, and one waitress too tired to care what they said. Alan sat already waiting, coat zipped to the chin, dark eyes sharper than Mitchell's ever were.

Koy didn't ease in. "You knew your brother was violent."

Alan sipped his coffee. "I knew he was unstable. There's a difference."

"He murdered his wife, his daughter... their dog. The state didn't think so, but you knew."

Alan didn't flinch. "Of course I knew. We all did."

That stopped Koy. "Then why didn't you say anything?"

He leaned forward. "Because it wasn't just him. Do you understand what I'm saying?"

"Help me."

Alan rubbed the bridge of his nose. "There are things in that family you don't speak about. Not just abuse. Things older than that house. My mother... her side's from Grayson County. There are old traditions. Old rites. They used to say our great-grandfather made pacts. Promises sealed in blood and buried under black walnut trees."

"Are you saying Mitchell was... cursed?"

"I'm saying Mitchell invited something in. When he was a teenager, he used to kill animals. My father covered it up. Then he started hurting women. The first girl he dated ended up in the ER. No charges...."

Koy sat back. "He brought something into that house. Or awakened it."

Alan nodded once. "He didn't create it, but he fed it. You've seen that tape. That wasn't just murder. That was... communion. There's a reason the house didn't fall apart. The reason it looked intact. Something held it together."

Koy swallowed. "You think it was more than a ghost."

"I think something old fed off what he did. And we all let it."

Koy didn't respond. The waitress poured more coffee and walked away.

Alan looked out the window. "I think the wrong person died first," he said. "And it stayed hungry."

# Chapter 34

He stared at the address again. It didn't make sense. Not unless someone, several someones, had helped Mitchell walk away from the wreckage he created in Bristol. Not unless the cover-up was deeper than anyone imagined.

Mitchell Owen was in Wilmington, North Carolina, living under the name Michael Owens. New address. New driver's license. New job in a family-run logistics company... and a new family. A wife. A little boy.

He didn't know what sickened him more: that Mitchell had escaped justice entirely, or that he'd replaced his old family like it was a busted appliance. How long until he gets tired of them and does the same thing?

He looked at the number. Alan had given it to him. He debated on whether he should call or not. Maybe he should let the authorities handle it. But everyone had done that. Instead of doing something, it was passed along to the next person. He thought of Morgan's sobs on video.

No. Petty or not, vengeful or not, someone needed to make him uncomfortable for a change. He dialed.

The phone rang longer than he expected. Then, click. A man answered, voice easy, warm, practiced. It was him. He heard him scream on that video.

"Hello?"

He didn't waste time with pleasantries. "Mitchell."

Silence. Then: "Sorry. Wrong number."

"You were smarter the first time," Koy said evenly. "I'm not a reporter. I'm not with the state. I'm the one who found what you left behind on Easton Avenue."

Another silence. This one longer. Then, low and slow: "Who is this?"

"You don't get to ask questions. You get to listen. I've

seen the tape. The one Morgan made. The one you never knew about."

"Whatever story you think you've got," Mitchell said, tone sharpening, "I'd be very careful about what you do with it."

"I already did something with it," Koy said. "I mailed five copies. One to the Attorney General. One to a national syndicate. Two to local law enforcement. And one to a lawyer who's not in your family's pocket."

The voice cracked, brittle around the edges now. "I don't know who you think you are, but you've got the wrong man. My name is...."

"I know your name," Koy cut in. "I know your wife's name. I know about your son. The one who looks almost exactly like Alida did, when she was his age."

"Shut your mouth!" Mitchell snapped.

Koy didn't flinch. "Is that what you said when Morgan begged you to stop? Is that what you said when you fed poison to your child?"

"You listen to me, you bastard..." The rage came in full now. Oh, there he was. There was the killer they knew. "You think I won't find you? You think you can crawl into my life and rip it open? I already paid. I started over. I have a right—"

"You forfeited rights when you killed your family," Koy said. "You don't get second chances." A vicious silence swallowed the line. Then, click. Dead air.

Koy sat motionless, phone still to his ear. He hadn't shouted. Hadn't lost control. But he knew... Mitchell had. He smiled. And now, there was proof. The real question was: how many people helped him start over?

And who else still had something to hide?

# CHAPTER 35

## Two weeks.

That's how long it had been since he mailed the tapes. He had sent them registered, certified, signed for. State police. Investigative journalists. Legal watchdogs. All the right channels.

And not one reply.

Not a single return call, email, or acknowledgment. He double-checked tracking numbers, every last one delivered. Some were signed for by name. Still nothing. The silence wasn't just suspicious. It was orchestrated.

He'd seen it before: wait it out, bury the footage, hope it disappears. Not this time. He wouldn't let it. Lisa had gone through hell. Morgan and Alida had been erased. He wasn't going to let the truth vanish with a few signed delivery receipts.

So, he took the thermonuclear route. He didn't like it, but there was no choice. *War it was.* He didn't want to choose proverbial violence, but it chose him.

He connected the VCR to a digital encoder, transferred the footage to MP4, and edited just enough to protect Lisa's address and voice from early sections. Then, he uploaded it as an unlisted video to see if it would get attention. The view count began to climb. Ten. Fifty. One hundred. But it wasn't fast enough.

So, he changed it. He posted the full, uncut version with a blunt title:

### "This Man Killed His Wife and Daughter. The Police Covered It Up."

He shared it to Reddit. Twitter. Facebook. He sent it to journalists directly with a single sentence:

**"Watch it. Then tell me nothing happened."**

Within twenty-four hours, the post exploded. Within forty-eight, the clip hit three million views. Comments flooded in.

**"How was this not investigated?"**
**"That poor little girl."**
**"I hope that bastard rots."**
**"This is the most disturbing thing I've ever watched."**
**"Find him. Find the people who let this happen."**

The major outlets couldn't ignore it. FOX ran a segment. Then BBC. Then CNN.

The thumbnail, Mitchell's face, blurry but recognizable, flashed across every screen in America. By the third day, the governor held a press conference. By the fourth, Mitchell was arrested in North Carolina.

He screamed the entire way into the back of the cruiser. The cameras captured every word. "This is a fucking lie! You people are idiots! I didn't do anything!"

But he did. And now everyone knew. He turned off the television that night and sat back in silence. The silence was broken.

Finally.

# Chapter 36

Lisa sat on the edge of Koy's guesthouse sofa, clutching her mug like it might shatter if she let go. The living room was dark, lit only by the flicker of the TV screen. Koy sat beside her, silent, remote in hand. Neither had spoken much that evening.

FOX ran the story on a loop. The anchors didn't hold back:

**"Viewers are warned this footage is disturbing."**
**"A woman begging for her life... a child**
**poisoned... a dog strangled..."**

They aired heavily blurred clips of Mitchell Owen's arrest: handcuffed, screaming, eyes wild. The network spliced in side-by-side comparisons, his current luxury home in North Carolina, complete with his second wife and two small stepchildren. Suburbia.

She stared as Mitchell was escorted past the reporters. His shirt was half-tucked. His face, red with rage.

"Do you deny the charges?"

"Of course I deny them, you fucking vultures!" he bellowed.

The moment froze on screen, captioned simply:

**"Arrest made in 2012 cold case murder of wife and daughter."**

She exhaled. Not a sob. Not relief, exactly. Just breath finally released after being held far too long. Koy muted the screen and turned to her. "You okay?"

She nodded slowly. "No. But it helps."

She wasn't sure how to describe it. It didn't undo anything. It wouldn't bring Morgan or Alida back. But the world knew now. Morgan wasn't crazy. She wasn't unstable.

She was terrified. She was hunted. And no one helped her when she begged for it.

But someone had now. Someone had listened. The moment that tape aired on national media, the world shifted. Mitchell's name, his real one, was all over the news. Talk shows debated the tragedy with righteous fury. Social media caught fire with the hashtag **#JusticeForMorganAndAlida.**

But it wasn't enough to see him dragged from a suburban home in Wilmington in handcuffs. Not for Koy. Not after everything she endured.

They weren't finished. Not after what Morgan went through. It wasn't enough until the people who helped bury the truth were exposed. And they had the names.

Detective Randall Gross was the first to fall. His handwritten notes, conveniently "lost" during the investigation, were found in a locked desk drawer in an old precinct filing room. They matched almost verbatim the Owen family's account. Gross didn't interview Morgan's sister. Or the neighbor who reported screams from Morgan's house once a week for six months. Under public pressure, the department launched an internal audit. Gross was terminated. His pension revoked.

Next was Principal Dawn Kesler. Emails between her and child protective services showed she'd never filed a formal report about Alida's bruises. Not once. But she'd suggested Morgan "seemed melodramatic" and "probably overprotective."

The real gut punch came when CPS records revealed Alida had missed school for five consecutive days before anyone bothered to ask where she was. Kesler resigned in disgrace.

CPS caseworker Richard Felton, who dismissed the abuse allegations after a single visit, citing "lack of concern from the child," was fired. A formal inquiry was opened into every case he'd touched over the last decade.

The Owen family's wealth no longer insulated them. Investigators traced wire transfers from patriarch Edwin Owen's trust to multiple members of the original investigation team. Bribes, paid to keep things "quiet." He claimed ignorance.

The IRS didn't. Edwin was indicted on charges of obstruction, fraud, and conspiracy to cover up a homicide.

Every public figure who'd called Morgan "troubled" or "problematic" was suddenly silent. Every professional who once painted her as "erratic" now offered apologies. But she didn't need their regret. She needed their replacement.

She watched in awe as a state senator introduced **The Owen Act**, a new law requiring independent oversight for all alleged domestic violence cases in which children are present. Mandatory CPS re-evaluations. Mandatory autopsy reviews for any suspected domestic death.

Morgan's name was in the preamble. Alida's name was in the title.

And Lisa, she stayed out of the spotlight. That was how she wanted it. They were never forgotten. And the world would never let it happen again.

# CHAPTER 37

She spent months in Koy's guesthouse. It was tucked at the back of a wooded lot, quiet and sun-dappled, with screened windows that let in fresh air and birdsong. The hospitality had been more than generous, meals, space, silence when she needed it, company when she didn't. She couldn't have asked for a more supportive host, or a more respectful one.

But still, she looked forward to her own home. And for the first time since Hal died, the word home didn't feel like a joke.

The strange numbness that had settled over her in the weeks after the wreck was gone. She felt present again, raw in some places, still tender in others, but awake. Alive. There were moments when she could almost recognize the woman she used to be. And that was enough, for now.

Koy's attorney had seen to it that the Owen family made things right, or at least as right as they could, where the house was concerned. They were forced to bring the structure up to code, replacing faulty systems, and securing a long-overdue inspection. Privately, Koy had mentioned the lawyer intimidated them so thoroughly they nearly handed over the deed. They gave her the money back and paid her hospital bills in exchange for silence. She agreed.

She now considered selling it. She didn't have to worry about passing the evil on. The house was clean. Not just physically. Not just with drywall replaced and air filters changed. But in some deeper, stranger way. Lighter.

There was no more scratching. No creaking from the basement. The malevolence, whatever had lived and festered in that house, was gone.

Her dreams had become just dreams again. When she could remember them at all, they were normal things: misplaced keys, awkward reunions, sometimes Hal's face at a distance. They were soft, not sharp. There were no monsters. No black-eyed women. No thundering whispers calling her name.

The house was quiet. And, for the first time in a very long time, so was she. There was no grand sense of victory. No epiphany or thunderclap of healing. Just... peace. And that was more than enough.

# Chapter 38

The memorial was simple. No procession. No podium. No speeches. Just a polished granite stone newly installed at the edge of a small local park, one Morgan had taken Alida to often, back when they lived quietly, and still had hope.

Lisa stood beside Koy in the spring sunlight, one hand on the black stone. It read:

> Morgan Elise Owen (1984–2012)
> Alida Grace Owen (2008–2012)
> Loved. Believed. Never forgotten.

Dozens of community members came. Most had never known the victims personally, but all had seen the footage. Some brought flowers. One child left a stuffed unicorn near the base of the marker.

Lisa spotted Sophia Allan off to the side. She didn't wave or smile. Just bowed her head. Regret clung to her like a shadow.

She didn't judge her. Not anymore. Some people looked away because it was easier. Because they weren't ready to face what might be real. But now, they didn't have a choice.

She knelt and touched the name "Alida" engraved in silver. She whispered something only the wind could hear. Koy waited a respectful distance back. He seemed to know better than to intrude.

When she stood, she looked up at the sky. It was wide open and bright. No clouds today.

"We did right by them," she said softly as she walked away.

He nodded. "Yes," he said. "We did."

# Epilogue

## *One Year Later*

She sat on the narrow steps of her new porch, warm coffee cupped in both hands. Her bare feet brushed the cool earth. A soft breeze stirred the treetops that surrounded the plot of land she now called home. It was quiet out here, no streetlights, no curious neighbors, no forgotten houses with locked rooms.

Just quiet.

The mobile home was perfect for her. It was roomy and pretty, and most importantly, new. No ghosts in the walls. No history clinging to the carpet. Just land and sky and time to breathe.

She believed in paranormal now. She didn't fear it. It was like grief, or memory, or weather, something that existed whether you liked it or not. Some places carried shadows. Some stories refused to stay buried. Some pain echoed after the scream. But not all ghosts were out for blood, and not all fear meant danger.

She'd lived in a haunted house. She'd been thrown, bloodied, terrified, and she'd survived. She'd helped a mother, and her child find peace. And when it was over, she didn't run.

She renovated. Fresh paint. New floors. Repairs the Owen family never bothered to make. She didn't erase what had happened there, but she made the house her own for the first time. She got her money back. And when it felt finished, settled, she sold it. Got more than she expected. Enough to buy this place. Enough to leave and enough to live on while she healed. She even got to save some.

The move outside town had been what she truly needed. No more creaking doors. No more cold spots. No more pretending to be okay while her soul unraveled. She woke up rested now. She cooked. She read again. She let the stillness heal what the storm had torn apart.

Koy still called every Sunday. Sometimes he came by with tea and some new story from the clinic. They didn't talk about the house. They didn't need to.

Once or twice, when the wind moved a certain way across the field, she thought she heard laughter. A little girl's voice. A dog's bark. And once, a white rose bloomed by the back fence, though she hadn't planted any.

She didn't flinch. She just smiled and whispered, "You're safe now."

Then she went back inside.

# ABOUT THE
# AUTHOR

L. Chambers Wright, writing also as Laura Wright, lives at the foot of the Appalachian Mountains, where the fog settles low and the stories never die. Her shelves creak under the weight of antique typewriters, and she keeps a collection of iron keys that unlock no known door. Her work explores forgotten roads, haunted bloodlines, and the quiet dread just past the tree line. Visit her at laurawrites.net.

www.ingramcontent.com/pod-product-compliance
Lightning Source LLC
Chambersburg PA
CBHW022033170626
46808CB00003B/1184